Hidenori Kusaka

I've completed my Alcremie collection! I have all the Sweets (seven types) and all the Creams (nine types) for a total of 63 in my storage system! I'm so happy. I have become a master stick spinner!

Satoshi Yamamoto

What I like best about *Pokémon: Sword & Shield*: ③ When the male Team Yell member throws his back out while cheering. That happened to me a few years ago at a punk concert! (LOL)

Pokémon
SWORD & SHIELD
5

STORY

Hidenori Kusaka

ART

Satoshi Yamamoto

Henry
SWORD

HENRY IS AN ARTISAN WHO UNDERSTANDS POKÉMON GEAR. HE IS THE DESCENDANT OF A RENOWNED SWORD-SMITH AND USES FAMILY SECRETS TO ENHANCE THE GEAR HE COMES ACROSS.

Casey
SHIELD

CASEY IS AN ACE COMPUTER HACKER WHO CAN CRACK ANY CODE AND GUESS ANY PASSWORD. SHE'S PROFESSOR MAGNOLIA'S ASSISTANT AND CHIPS IN AS THE TEAM'S DATA ANALYST.

The Story So Far

UPON ARRIVING IN THE GALAR REGION, MARVIN SEES A DYNAMAXED POKÉMON AND FALLS OFF A CLIFF! HE IS SAVED BY HENRY SWORD AND CASEY SHIELD AND JOINS THEM ON THEIR JOURNEY TO COMPLETE THEIR GYM CHALLENGE AND DISCOVER THE SECRET OF DYNAMAXING WITH PROFESSOR MAGNOLIA. HENRY AND HIS FRIENDS THEN GET THE OPPORTUNITY TO VISIT THE HAMMERLOCKE VAULT, WHERE THEY LEARN ABOUT THE FOUNDING OF THE GALAR REGION FROM A TAPESTRY.

Marvin

A ROOKIE TRAINER WHO RECENTLY MOVED TO GALAR. HE'S EXCITED TO LEARN EVERYTHING HE CAN ABOUT POKÉMON!

Professor Magnolia

A FAMED RESEARCHER WHO STUDIES DYNAMAXING, THE GIGANTIFICATION OF POKÉMON.

Leon

LEON IS THE BEST TRAINER IN GALAR. HE'S THE UNDEFEATED CHAMPION!

Sonia

PROFESSOR MAGNOLIA'S GRANDDAUGHTER AND LEON'S CHILDHOOD FRIEND. SHE'S HELPING THE PROFESSOR INVESTIGATE THE GALAR REGION!

CONTENTS

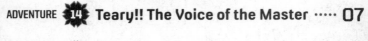

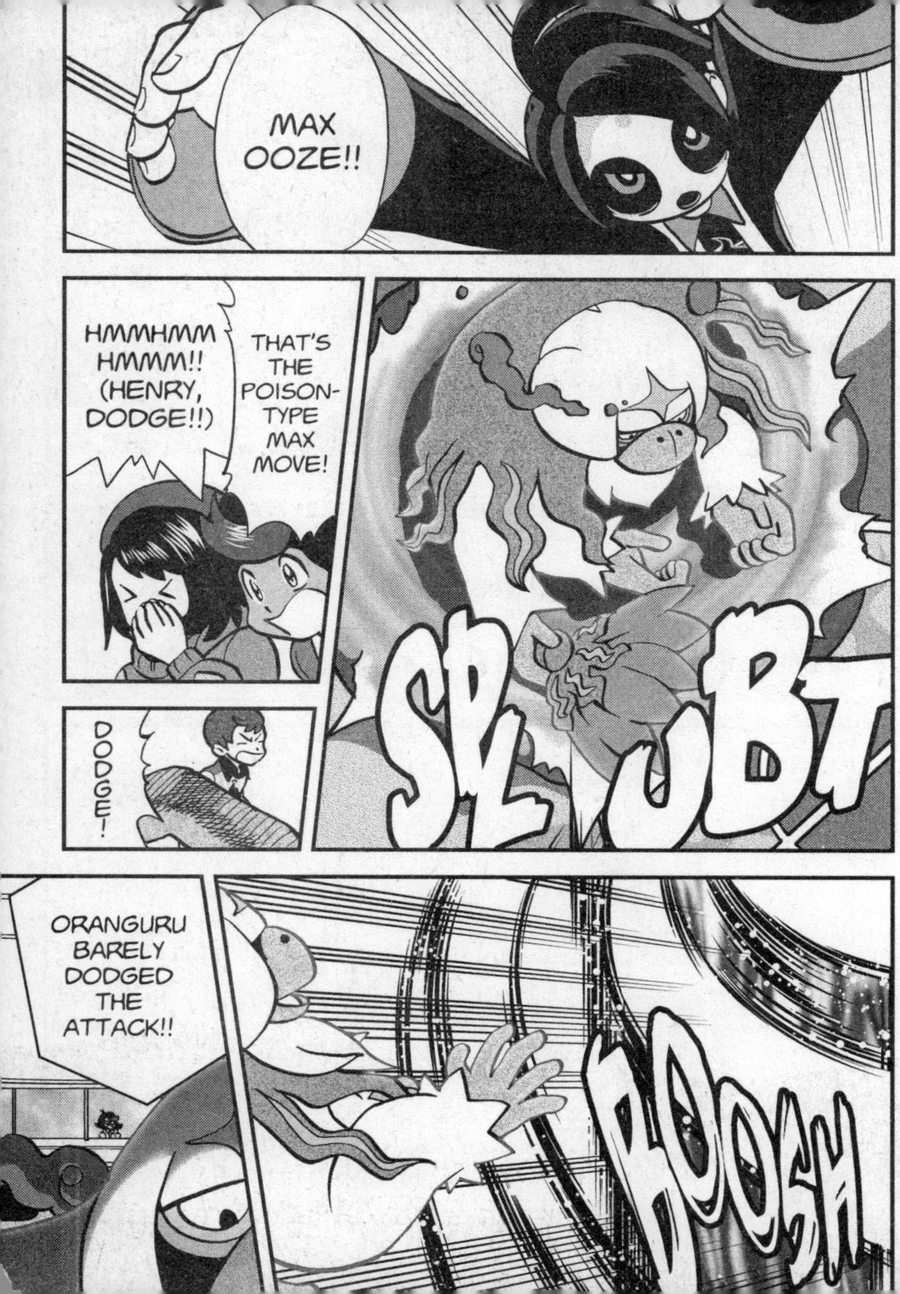
MAX OOZE!!
SPLUBT
THAT'S THE POISON-TYPE MAX MOVE!
HMMHMM HMMM!! (HENRY, DODGE!!)
DODGE!
ORANGURU BARELY DODGED THE ATTACK!!
FOOSH

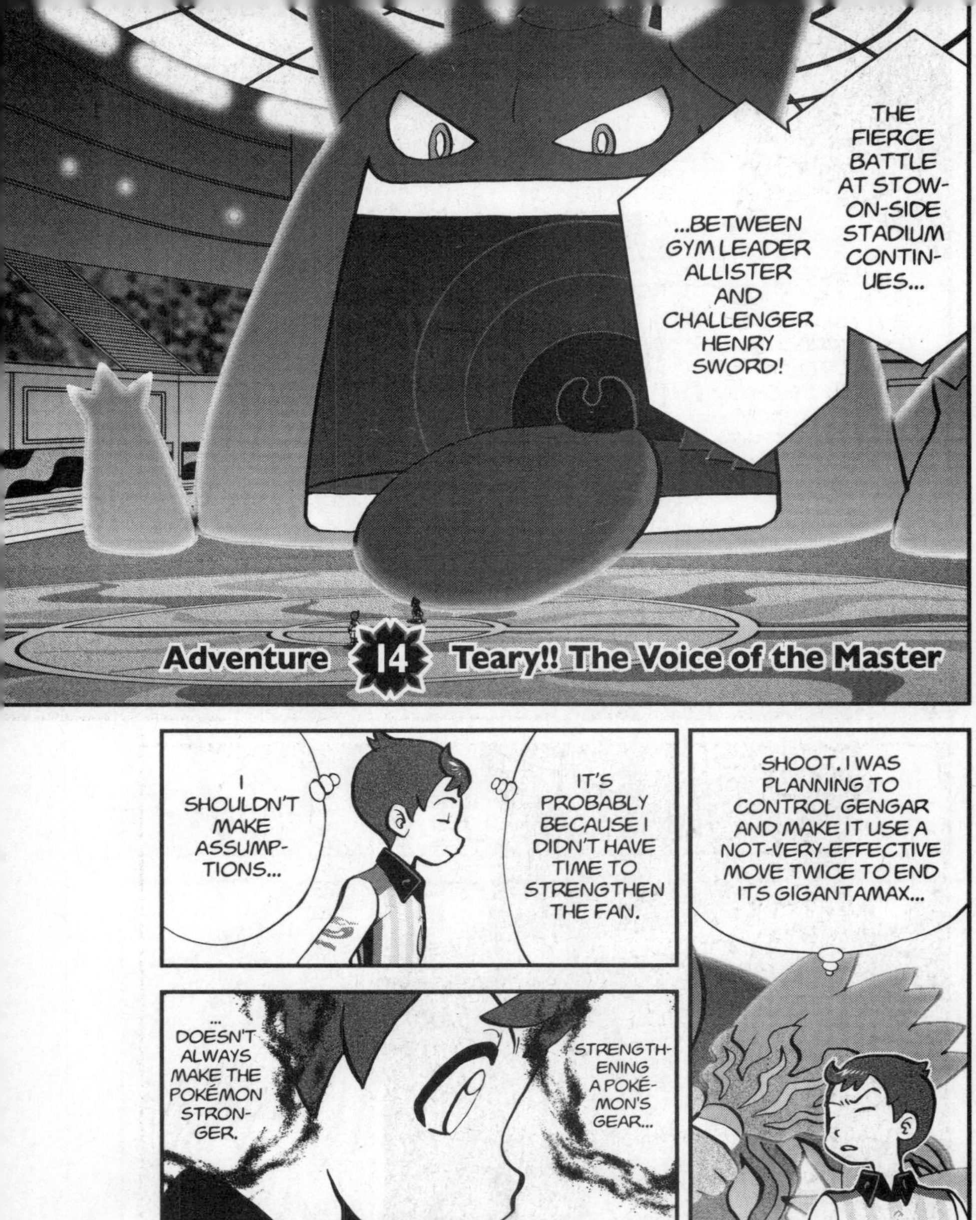
THE FIERCE BATTLE AT STOW-ON-SIDE STADIUM CONTIN-UES...
...BETWEEN GYM LEADER ALLISTER AND CHALLENGER HENRY SWORD!
Adventure 14 Teary!! The Voice of the Master
SHOOT. I WAS PLANNING TO CONTROL GENGAR AND MAKE IT USE A NOT-VERY-EFFECTIVE MOVE TWICE TO END ITS GIGANTAMAX...
IT'S PROBABLY BECAUSE I DIDN'T HAVE TIME TO STRENGTHEN THE FAN.
I SHOULDN'T MAKE ASSUMP-TIONS...
STRENGTH-ENING A POKÉ-MON'S GEAR...
...DOESN'T ALWAYS MAKE THE POKÉMON STRON-GER.

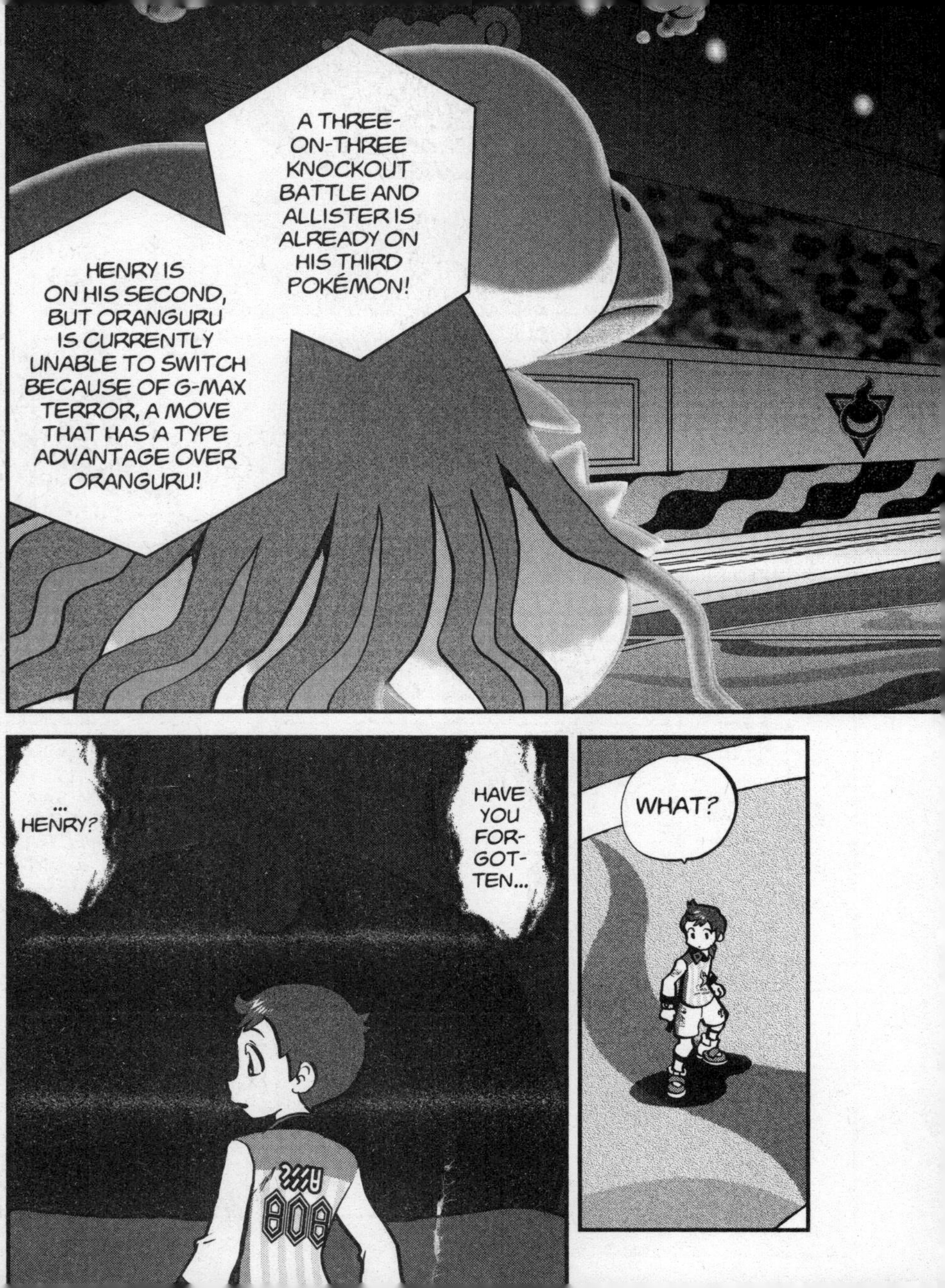
A THREE-ON-THREE KNOCKOUT BATTLE AND ALLISTER IS ALREADY ON HIS THIRD POKÉMON!
HENRY IS ON HIS SECOND, BUT ORANGURU IS CURRENTLY UNABLE TO SWITCH BECAUSE OF G-MAX TERROR, A MOVE THAT HAS A TYPE ADVANTAGE OVER ORANGURU!
WHAT?
HAVE YOU FORGOTTEN...
...HENRY?

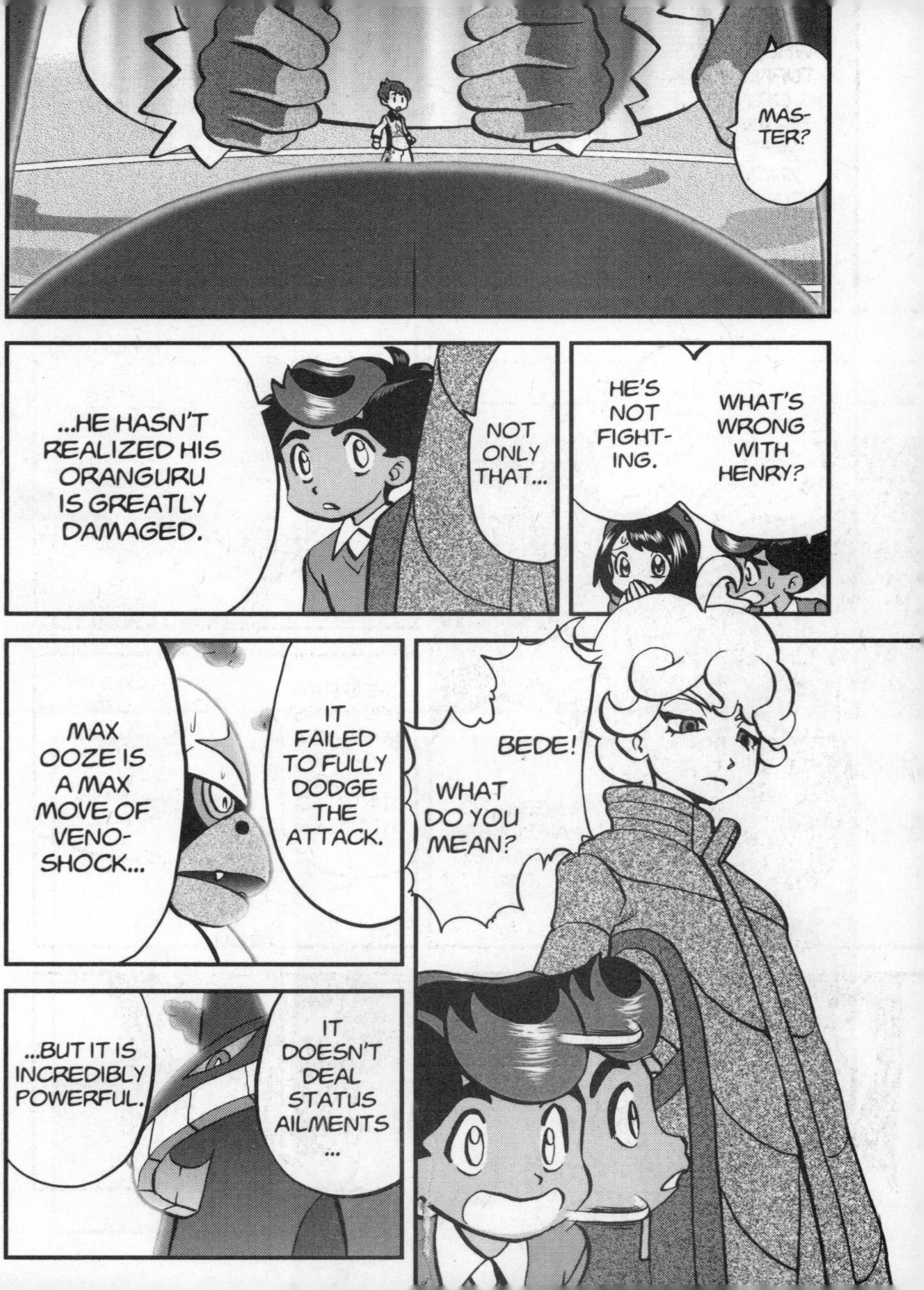
MAS-TER?
WHAT'S WRONG WITH HENRY?
HE'S NOT FIGHT-ING.
NOT ONLY THAT...
...HE HASN'T REALIZED HIS ORANGURU IS GREATLY DAMAGED.
BEDE! WHAT DO YOU MEAN?
IT FAILED TO FULLY DODGE THE ATTACK.
MAX OOZE IS A MAX MOVE OF VENO-SHOCK...
IT DOESN'T DEAL STATUS AILMENTS...
...BUT IT IS INCREDIBLY POWERFUL.

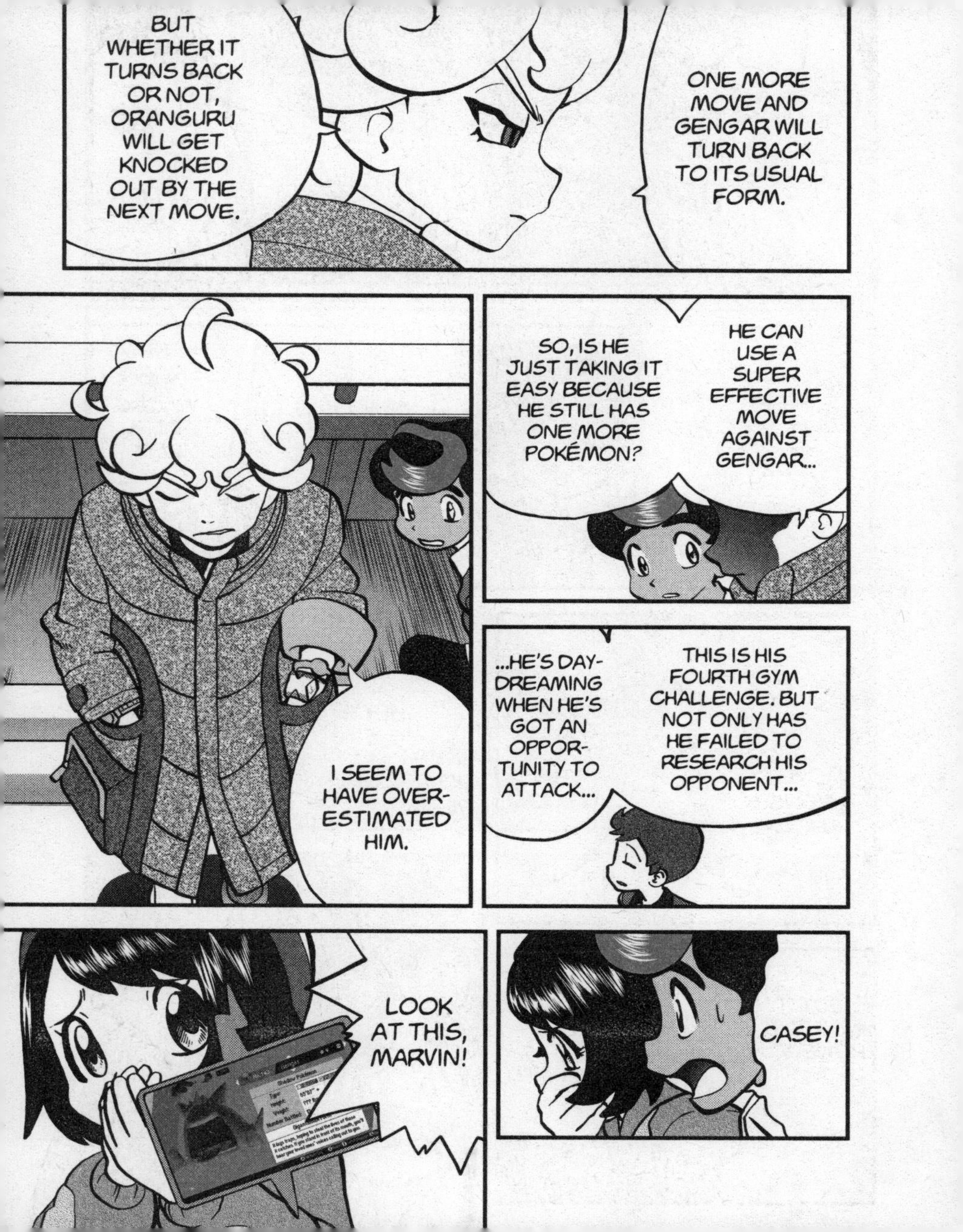
ONE MORE MOVE AND GENGAR WILL TURN BACK TO ITS USUAL FORM.
BUT WHETHER IT TURNS BACK OR NOT, ORANGURU WILL GET KNOCKED OUT BY THE NEXT MOVE.
HE CAN USE A SUPER EFFECTIVE MOVE AGAINST GENGAR...
SO, IS HE JUST TAKING IT EASY BECAUSE HE STILL HAS ONE MORE POKÉMON?
THIS IS HIS FOURTH GYM CHALLENGE. BUT NOT ONLY HAS HE FAILED TO RESEARCH HIS OPPONENT...
...HE'S DAY-DREAMING WHEN HE'S GOT AN OPPOR-TUNITY TO ATTACK...
I SEEM TO HAVE OVER-ESTIMATED HIM.
CASEY!
LOOK AT THIS, MARVIN!

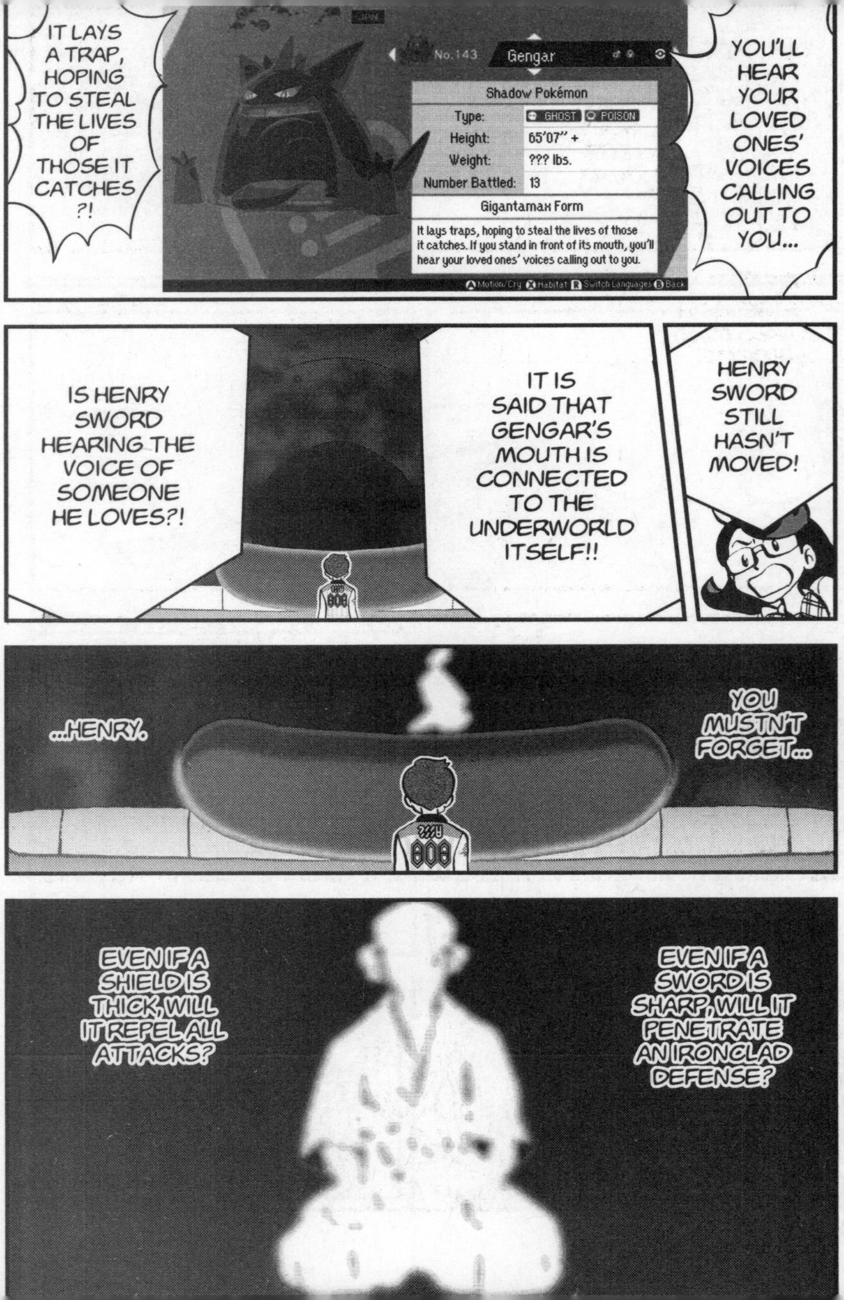

YOU'LL HEAR YOUR LOVED ONES' VOICES CALLING OUT TO YOU...
No.143
Gengar
Shadow Pokémon
Type: GHOST POISON
Height: 65'07" +
Weight: ??? lbs.
Number Battled: 13
Gigantamax Form
It lays traps, hoping to steal the lives of those it catches. If you stand in front of its mouth, you'll hear your loved ones' voices calling out to you.
Motion/Cry Habitat Switch Languages Back
IT LAYS A TRAP, HOPING TO STEAL THE LIVES OF THOSE IT CATCHES ?!
HENRY SWORD STILL HASN'T MOVED!
IT IS SAID THAT GENGAR'S MOUTH IS CONNECTED TO THE UNDERWORLD ITSELF!!
IS HENRY SWORD HEARING THE VOICE OF SOMEONE HE LOVES?!
YOU MUSTN'T FORGET...
...HENRY.
EVEN IF A SWORD IS SHARP, WILL IT PENETRATE AN IRONCLAD DEFENSE?
EVEN IF A SHIELD IS THICK, WILL IT REPEL ALL ATTACKS?

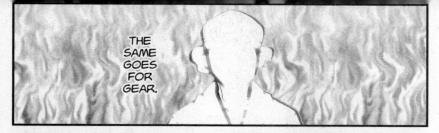

THE SAME GOES FOR GEAR.
THERE ARE MANY WAYS TO STRENGTHEN GEAR.
STRENGTH TAKES MANY FORMS.
YOU MUST CHERISH WEAKNESS...
...AND TRY TO SUPPLEMENT IT.
WEAKNESS IS NOT SOMETHING TO BE ASHAMED OF.
THOSE WHO REJECT IT WILL NEVER MASTER GEAR, OR POKÉMON.

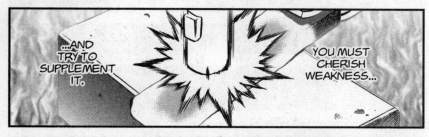

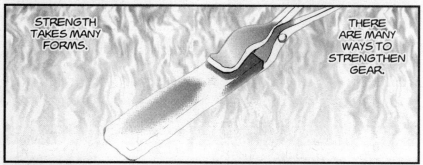

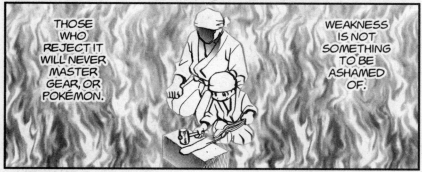

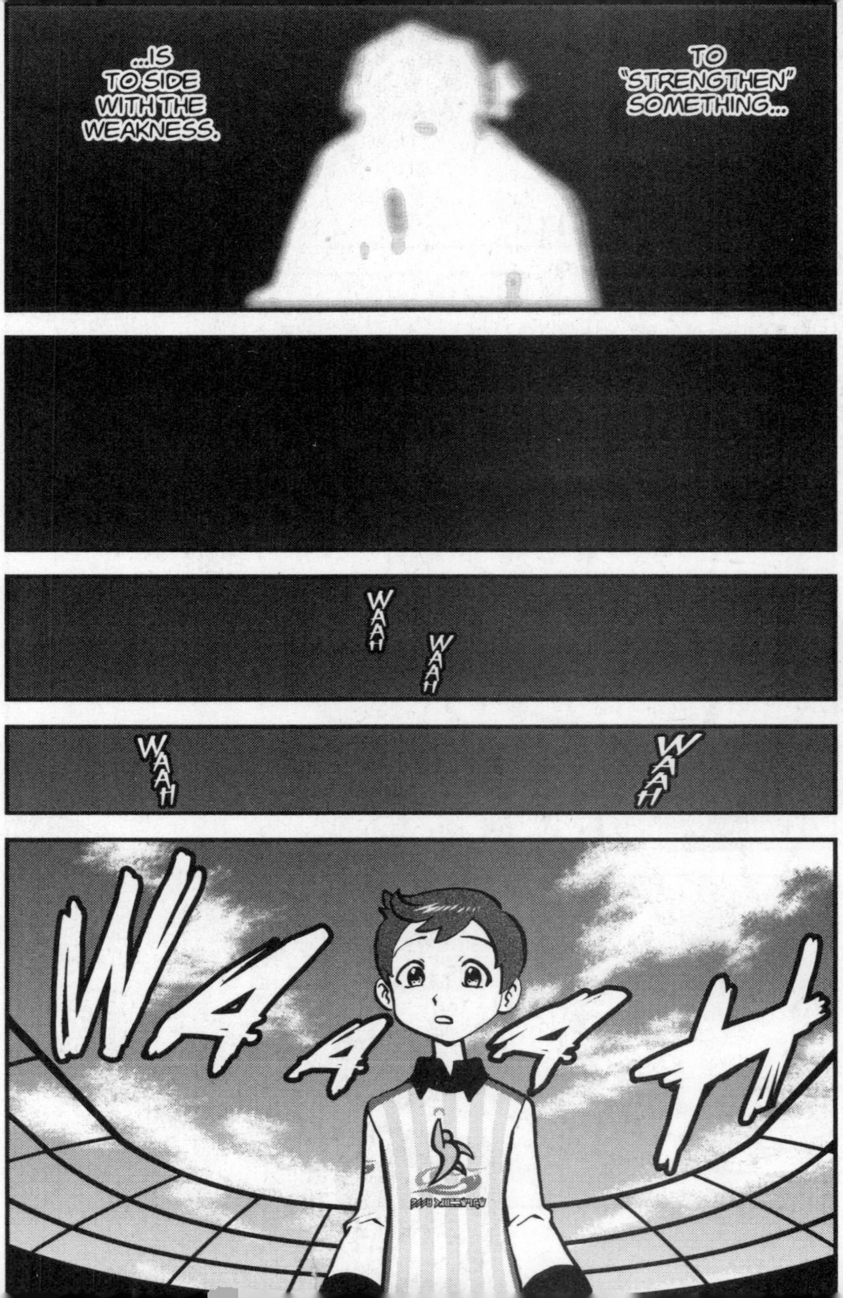

TO "STRENGTHEN" SOMETHING...
...IS TO SIDE WITH THE WEAKNESS.
WAAH
WAAH
WAAH
WAAH
WAAAH

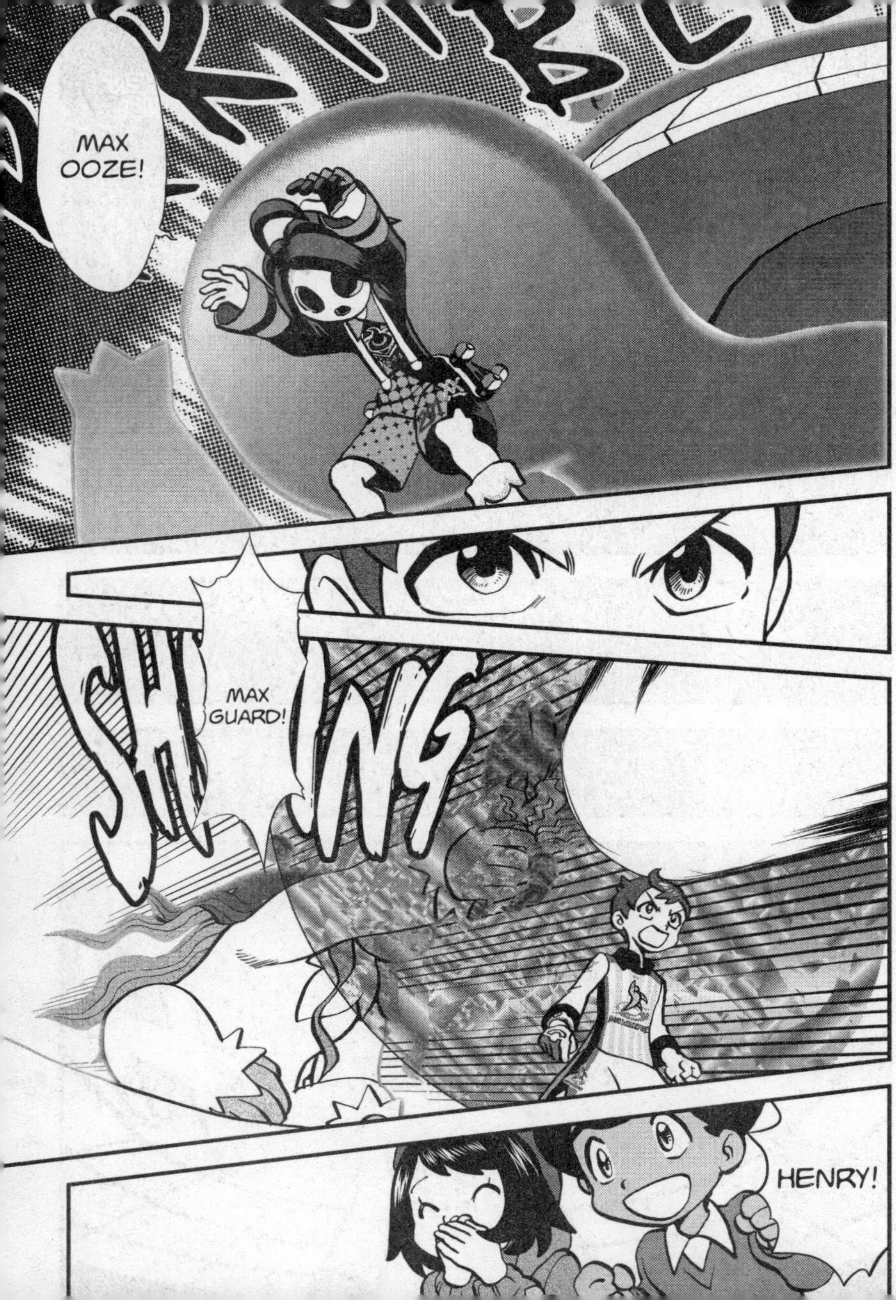
MAX OOZE!
MAX GUARD!
SHING
HENRY!

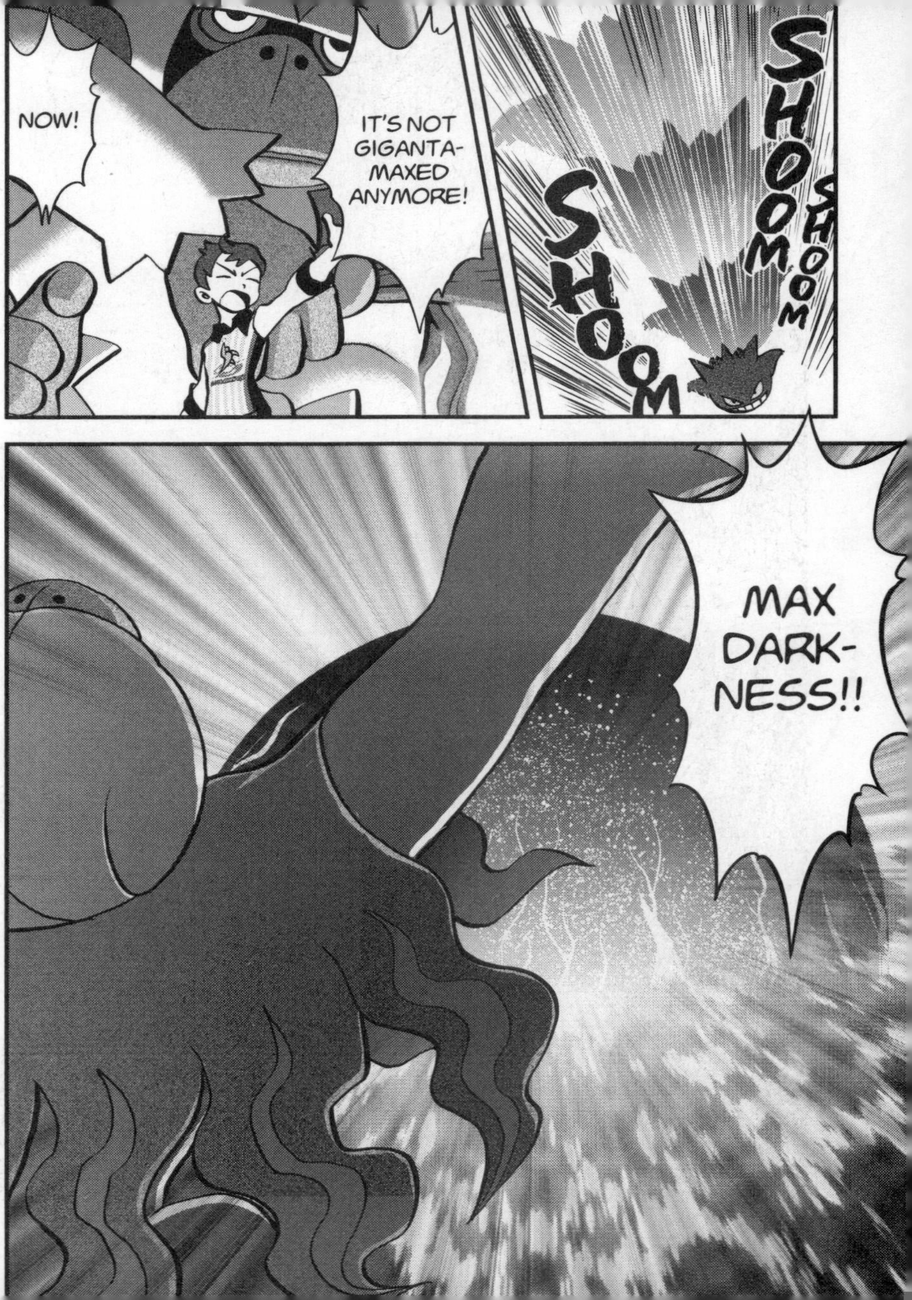
SHOOM
SHOOM
SHOOM
IT'S NOT GIGANTA-MAXED ANYMORE!
NOW!
MAX DARK-NESS!!

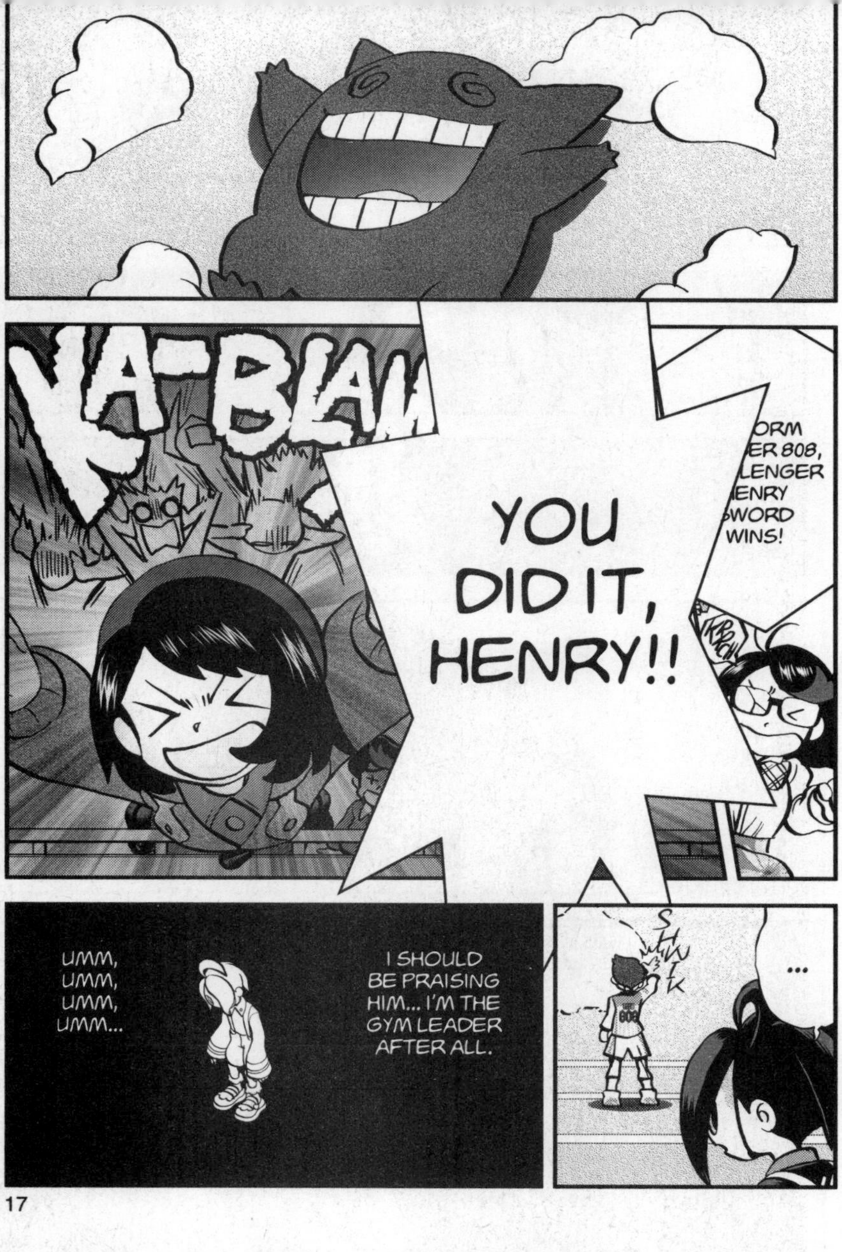
ORM ER 808, LENGER ENRY SWORD WINS!
YOU DID IT, HENRY!!
A-BLAM
SHWIK
...
I SHOULD BE PRAISING HIM... I'M THE GYM LEADER AFTER ALL.
UMM, UMM, UMM, UMM...

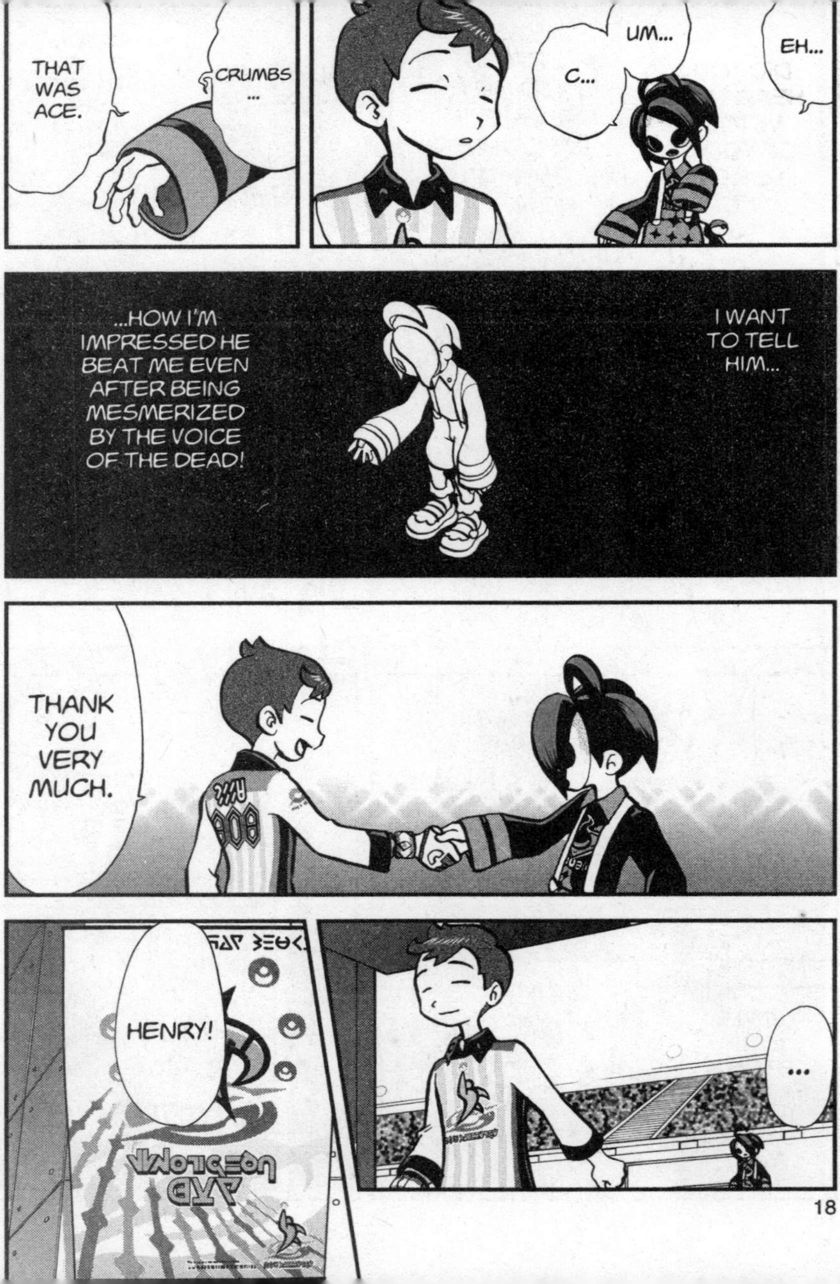
EH...
UM...
C...
CRUMBS ...
THAT WAS ACE.
I WANT TO TELL HIM...
...HOW I'M IMPRESSED HE BEAT ME EVEN AFTER BEING MESMERIZED BY THE VOICE OF THE DEAD!
THANK YOU VERY MUCH.
...
HENRY!

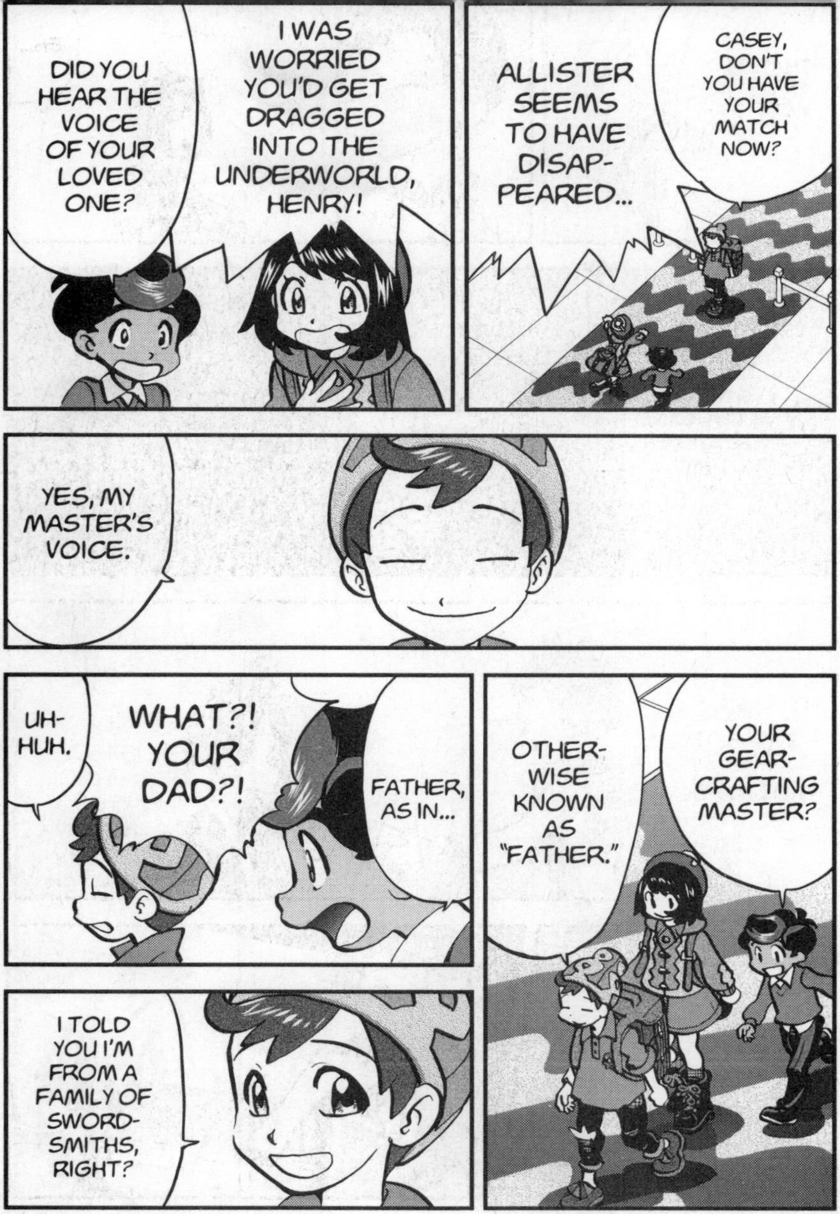
CASEY, DON'T YOU HAVE YOUR MATCH NOW?
ALLISTER SEEMS TO HAVE DISAP-PEARED...
I WAS WORRIED YOU'D GET DRAGGED INTO THE UNDERWORLD, HENRY!
DID YOU HEAR THE VOICE OF YOUR LOVED ONE?
YES, MY MASTER'S VOICE.
YOUR GEAR-CRAFTING MASTER?
OTHER-WISE KNOWN AS "FATHER."
FATHER, AS IN...
WHAT?! YOUR DAD?!
UH-HUH.
I TOLD YOU I'M FROM A FAMILY OF SWORD-SMITHS, RIGHT?

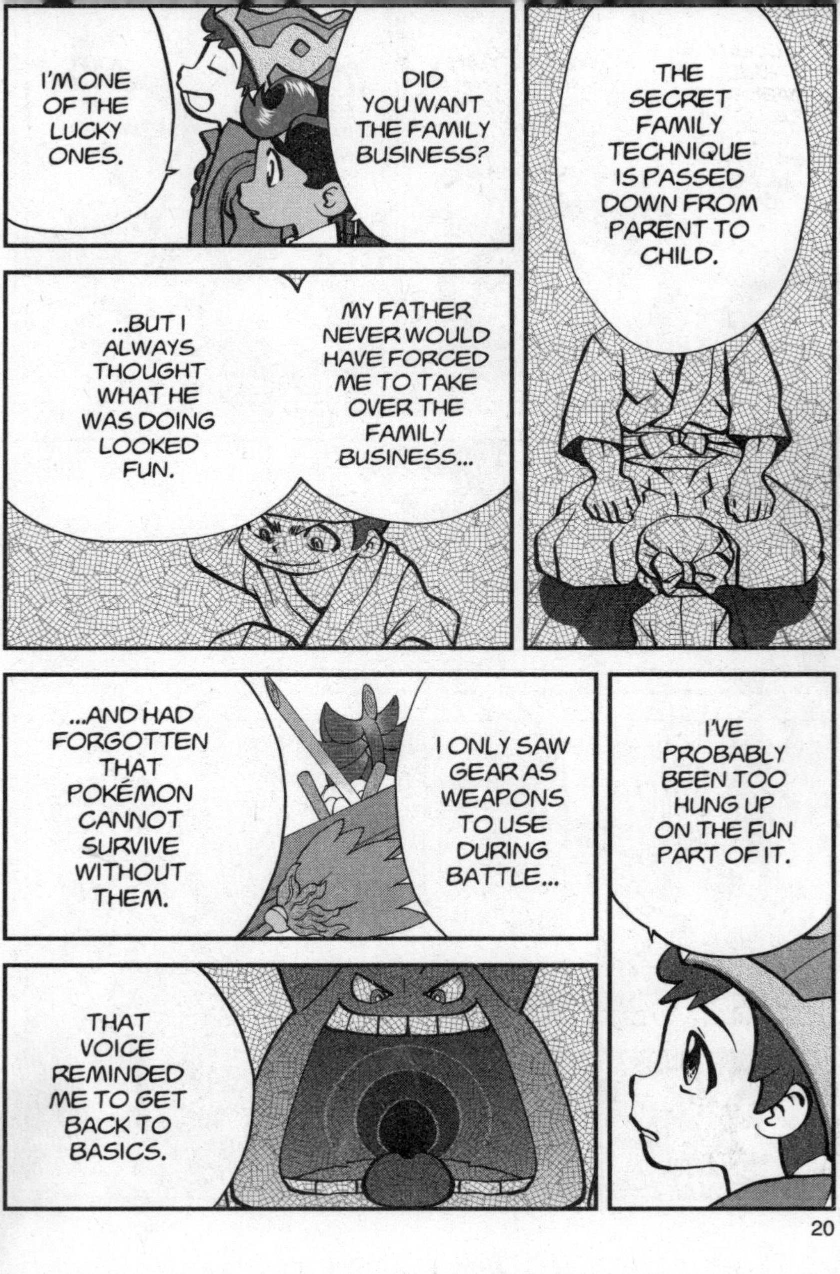
THE SECRET FAMILY TECHNIQUE IS PASSED DOWN FROM PARENT TO CHILD.
DID YOU WANT THE FAMILY BUSINESS?
I'M ONE OF THE LUCKY ONES.
MY FATHER NEVER WOULD HAVE FORCED ME TO TAKE OVER THE FAMILY BUSINESS...
...BUT I ALWAYS THOUGHT WHAT HE WAS DOING LOOKED FUN.
I'VE PROBABLY BEEN TOO HUNG UP ON THE FUN PART OF IT.
I ONLY SAW GEAR AS WEAPONS TO USE DURING BATTLE...
...AND HAD FORGOTTEN THAT POKÉMON CANNOT SURVIVE WITHOUT THEM.
THAT VOICE REMINDED ME TO GET BACK TO BASICS.

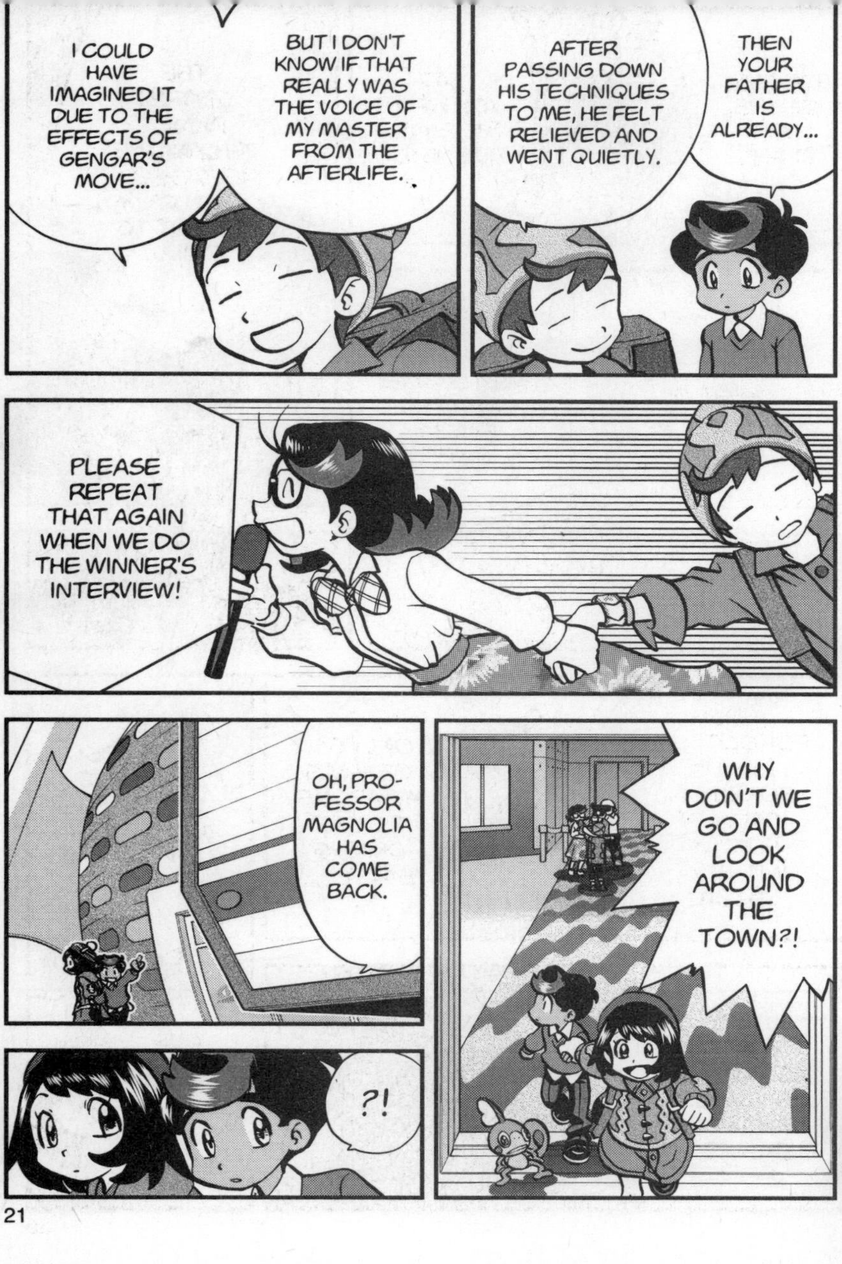
THEN YOUR FATHER IS ALREADY...
AFTER PASSING DOWN HIS TECHNIQUES TO ME, HE FELT RELIEVED AND WENT QUIETLY.
BUT I DON'T KNOW IF THAT REALLY WAS THE VOICE OF MY MASTER FROM THE AFTERLIFE...
I COULD HAVE IMAGINED IT DUE TO THE EFFECTS OF GENGAR'S MOVE...
PLEASE REPEAT THAT AGAIN WHEN WE DO THE WINNER'S INTERVIEW!
WHY DON'T WE GO AND LOOK AROUND THE TOWN?!
OH, PRO-FESSOR MAGNOLIA HAS COME BACK.
?!

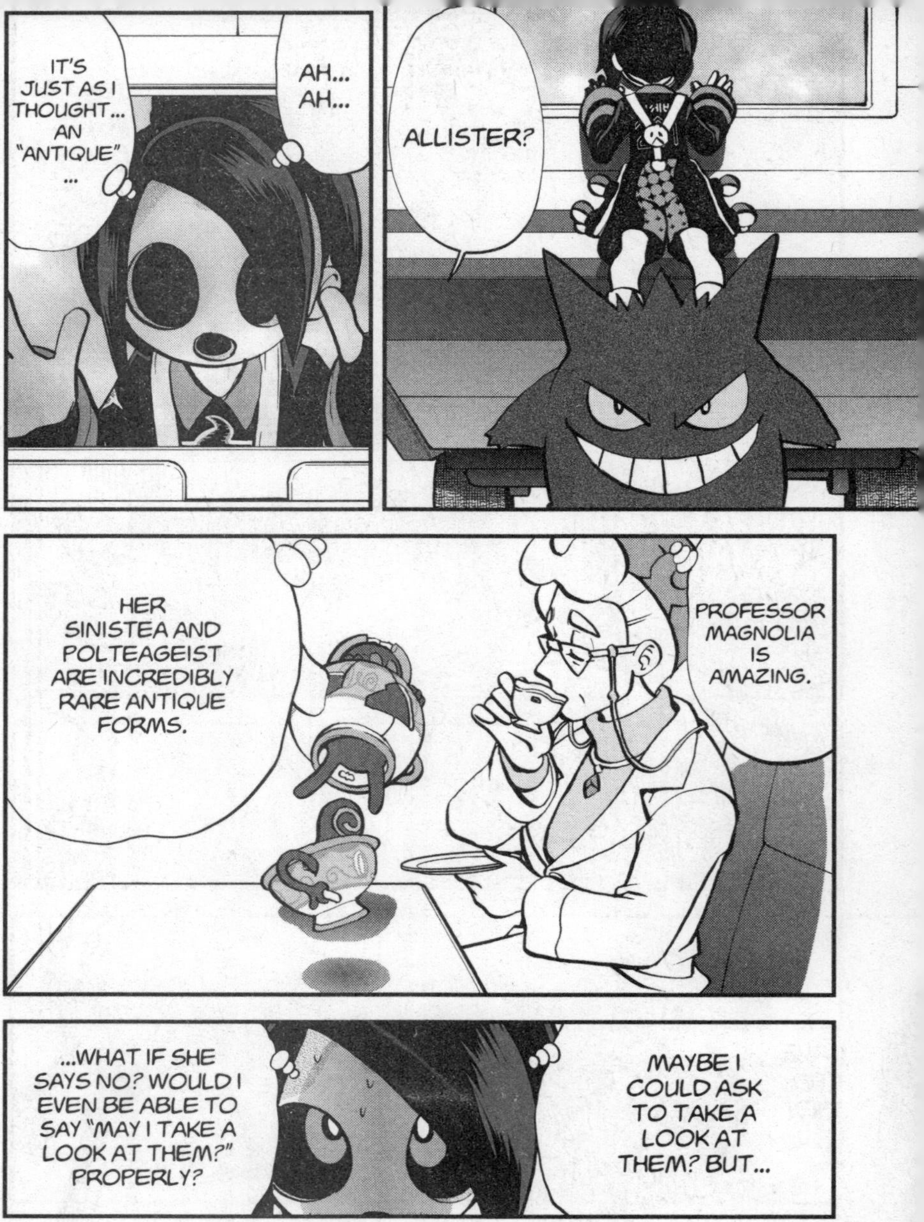
ALLISTER?
AH... AH...
IT'S JUST AS I THOUGHT... AN "ANTIQUE" ...
PROFESSOR MAGNOLIA IS AMAZING.
HER SINISTEA AND POLTEAGEIST ARE INCREDIBLY RARE ANTIQUE FORMS.
MAYBE I COULD ASK TO TAKE A LOOK AT THEM? BUT...
...WHAT IF SHE SAYS NO? WOULD I EVEN BE ABLE TO SAY "MAY I TAKE A LOOK AT THEM?" PROPERLY?

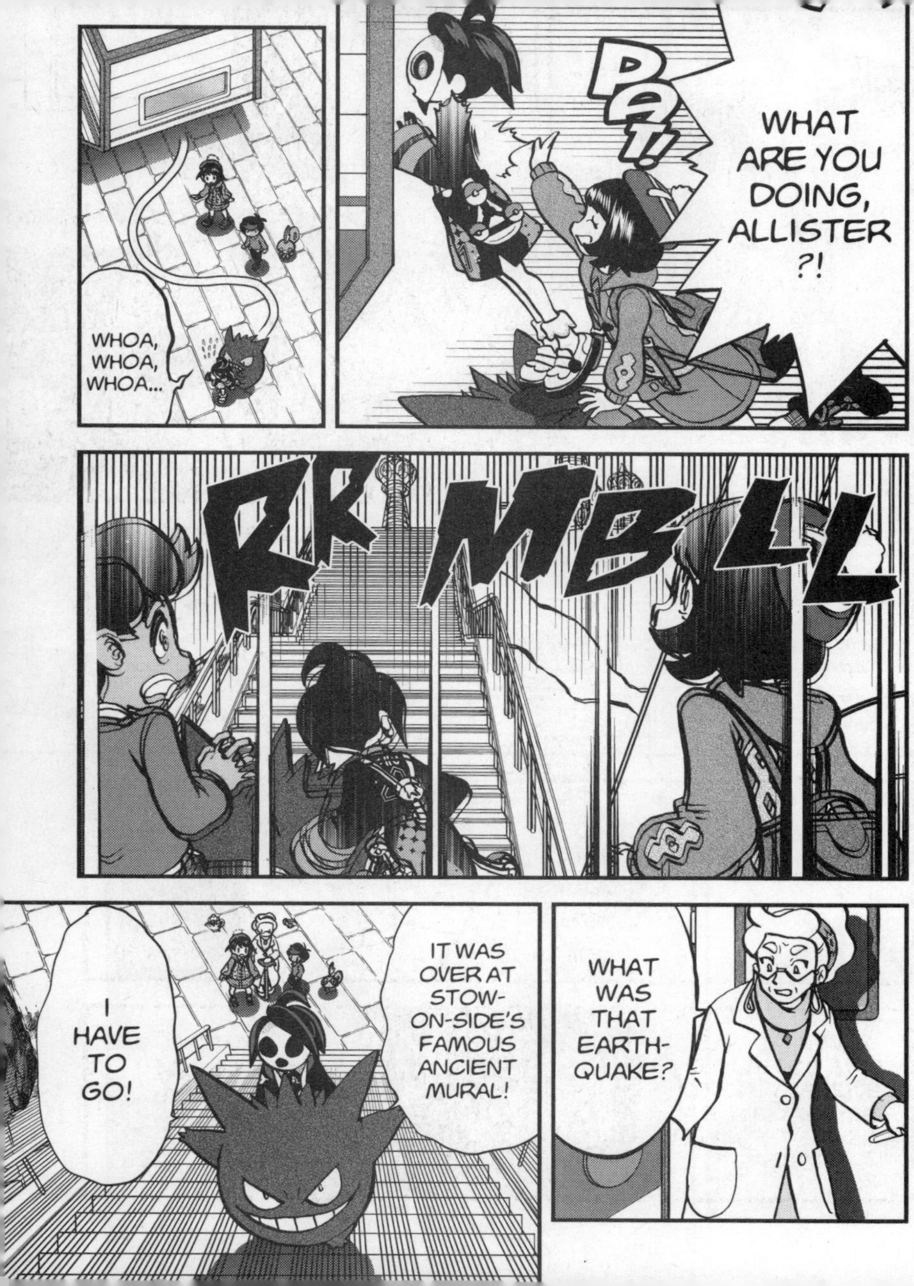
PAT!!
WHAT ARE YOU DOING, ALLISTER?!
WHOA, WHOA, WHOA...
RRMBLL
WHAT WAS THAT EARTHQUAKE?
IT WAS OVER AT STOW-ON-SIDE'S FAMOUS ANCIENT MURAL!
I HAVE TO GO!

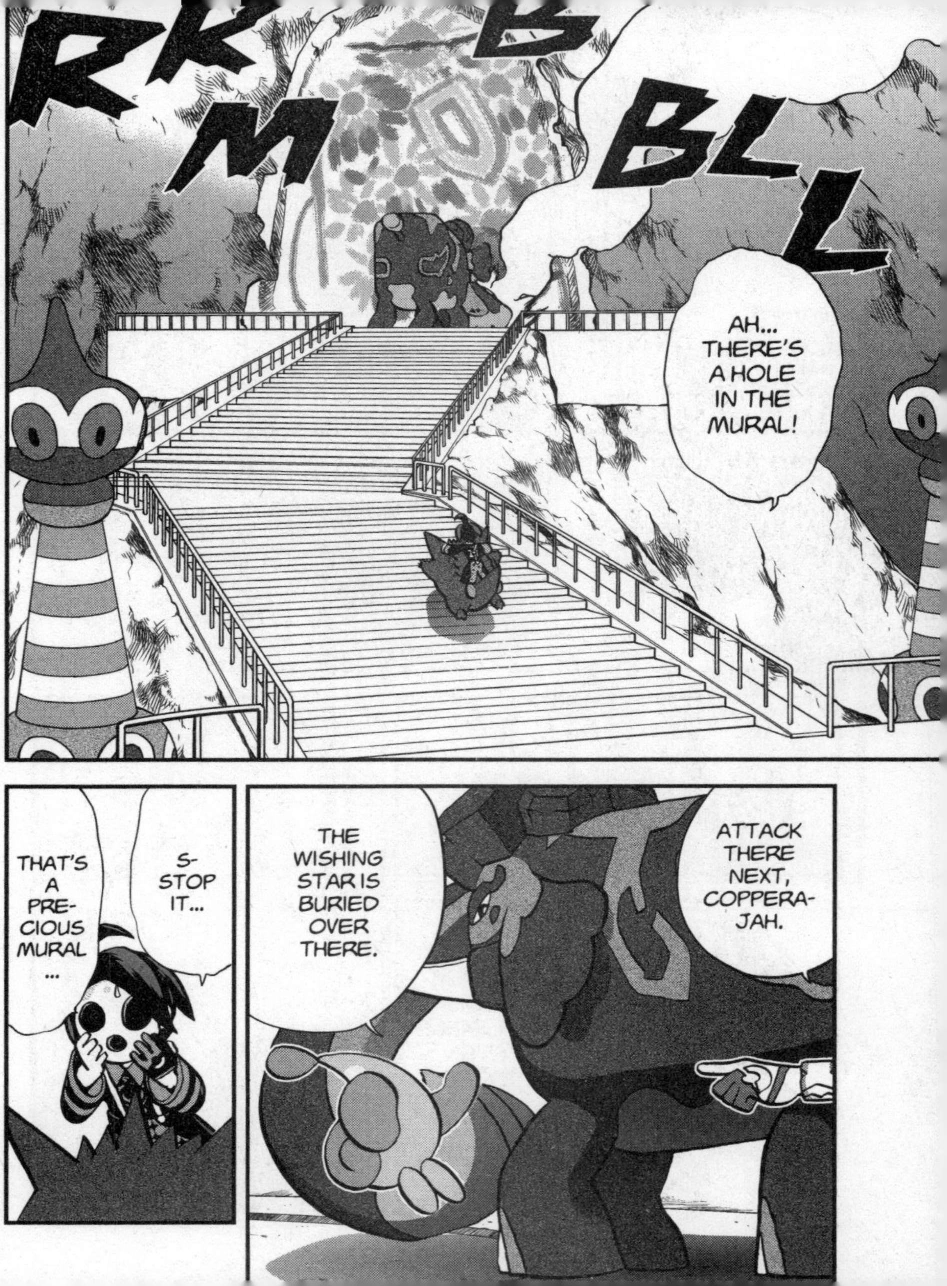
RKMBBLL
AH... THERE'S A HOLE IN THE MURAL!
ATTACK THERE NEXT, COPPERAJAH.
THE WISHING STAR IS BURIED OVER THERE.
S-STOP IT...
THAT'S A PRECIOUS MURAL...

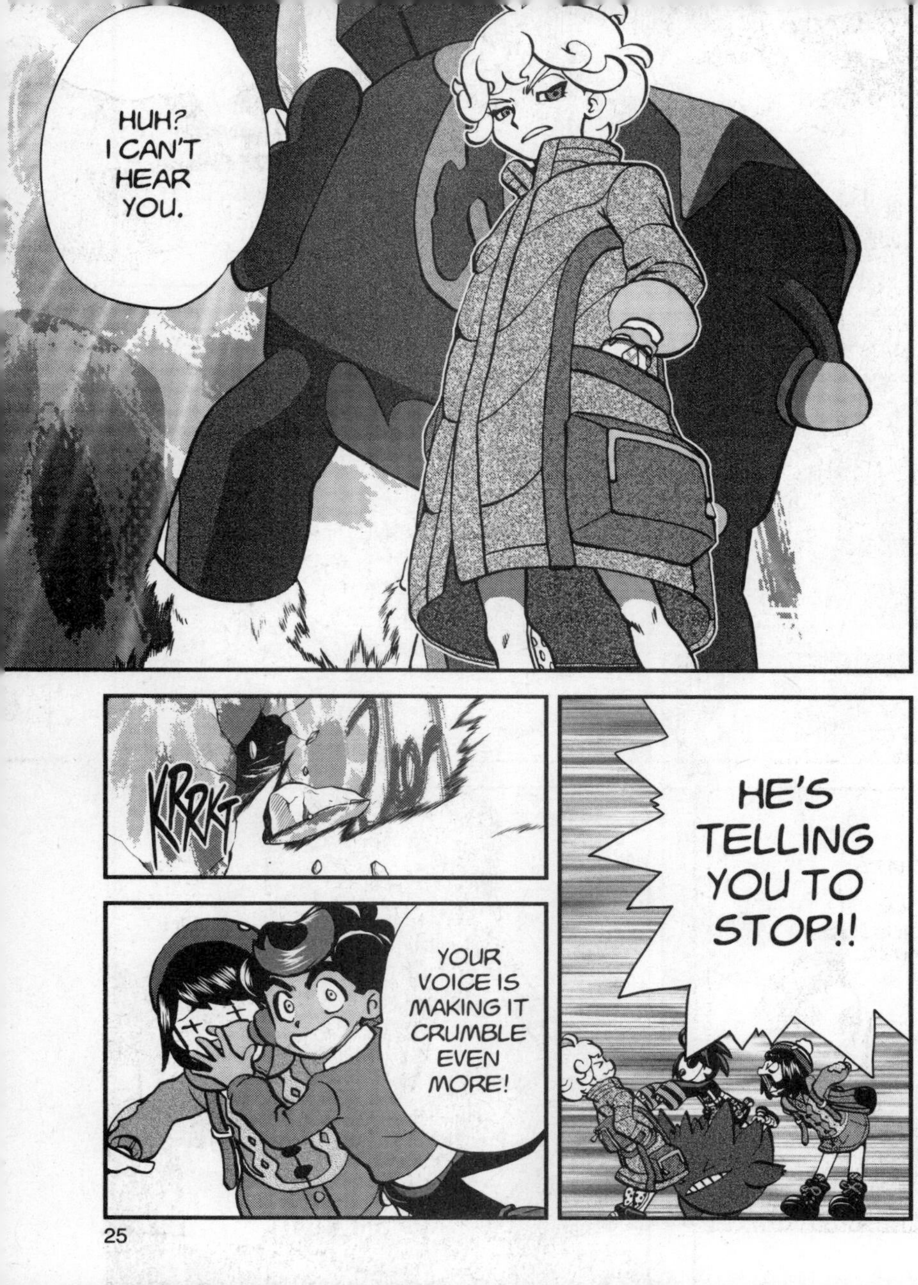
HUH? I CAN'T HEAR YOU.
HE'S TELLING YOU TO STOP!!
KRRKT
YOUR VOICE IS MAKING IT CRUMBLE EVEN MORE!

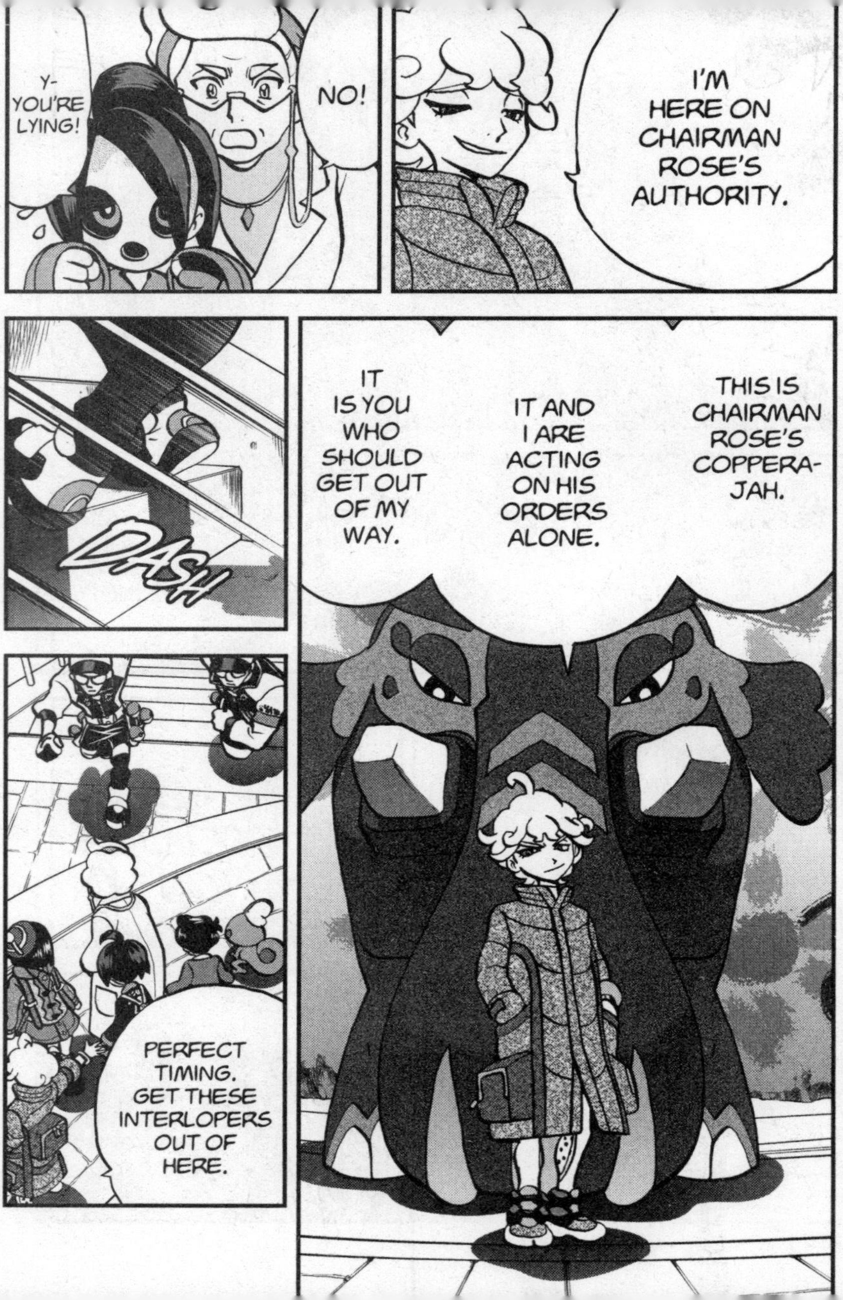
I'M HERE ON CHAIRMAN ROSE'S AUTHORITY.
NO!
Y-YOU'RE LYING!
THIS IS CHAIRMAN ROSE'S COPPERA-JAH.
IT AND I ARE ACTING ON HIS ORDERS ALONE.
IT IS YOU WHO SHOULD GET OUT OF MY WAY.
DASH
PERFECT TIMING. GET THESE INTERLOPERS OUT OF HERE.

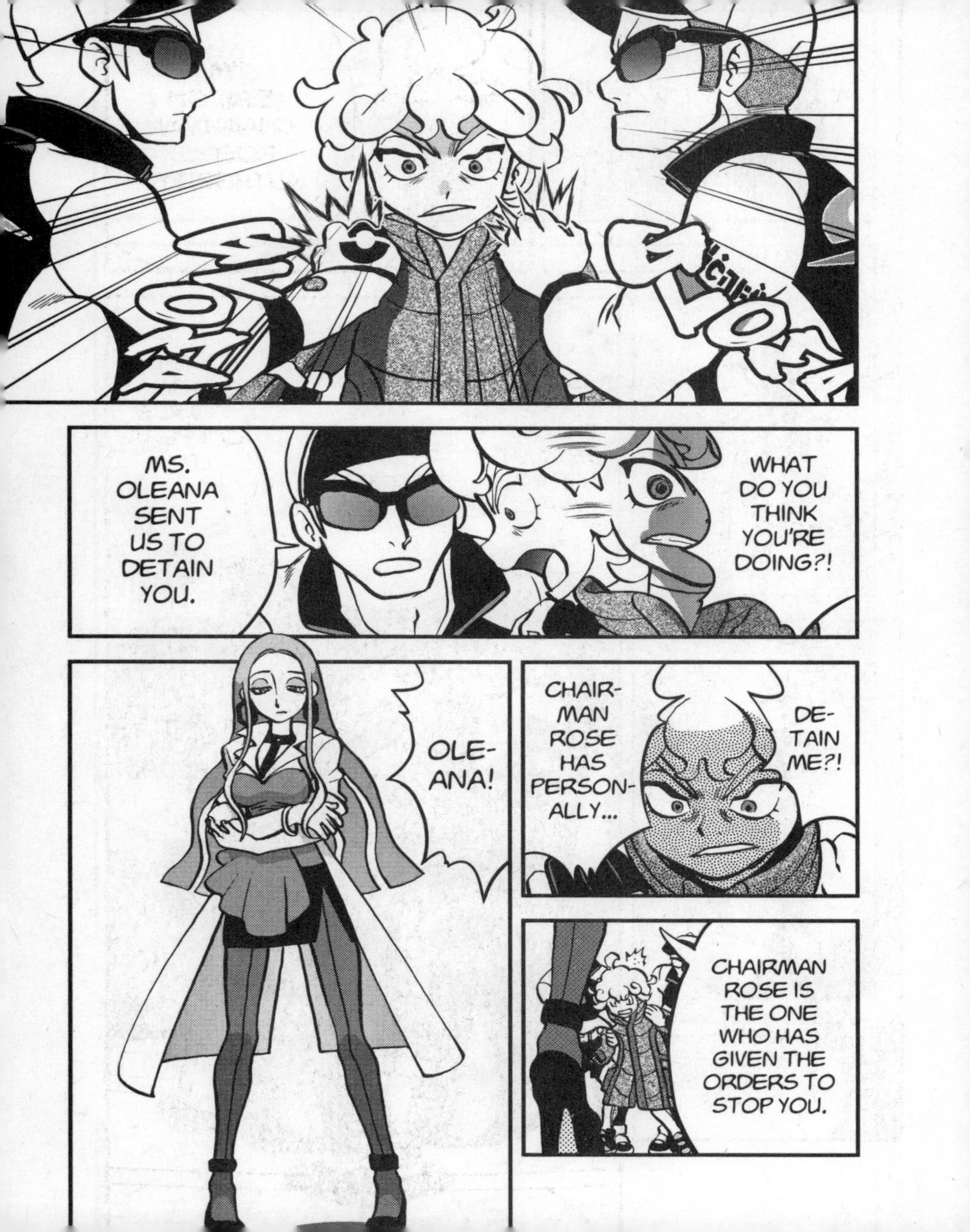
WHAT DO YOU THINK YOU'RE DOING?!
MS. OLEANA SENT US TO DETAIN YOU.
DE-TAIN ME?!
CHAIR-MAN ROSE HAS PERSON-ALLY...
CHAIRMAN ROSE IS THE ONE WHO HAS GIVEN THE ORDERS TO STOP YOU.
OLE-ANA!

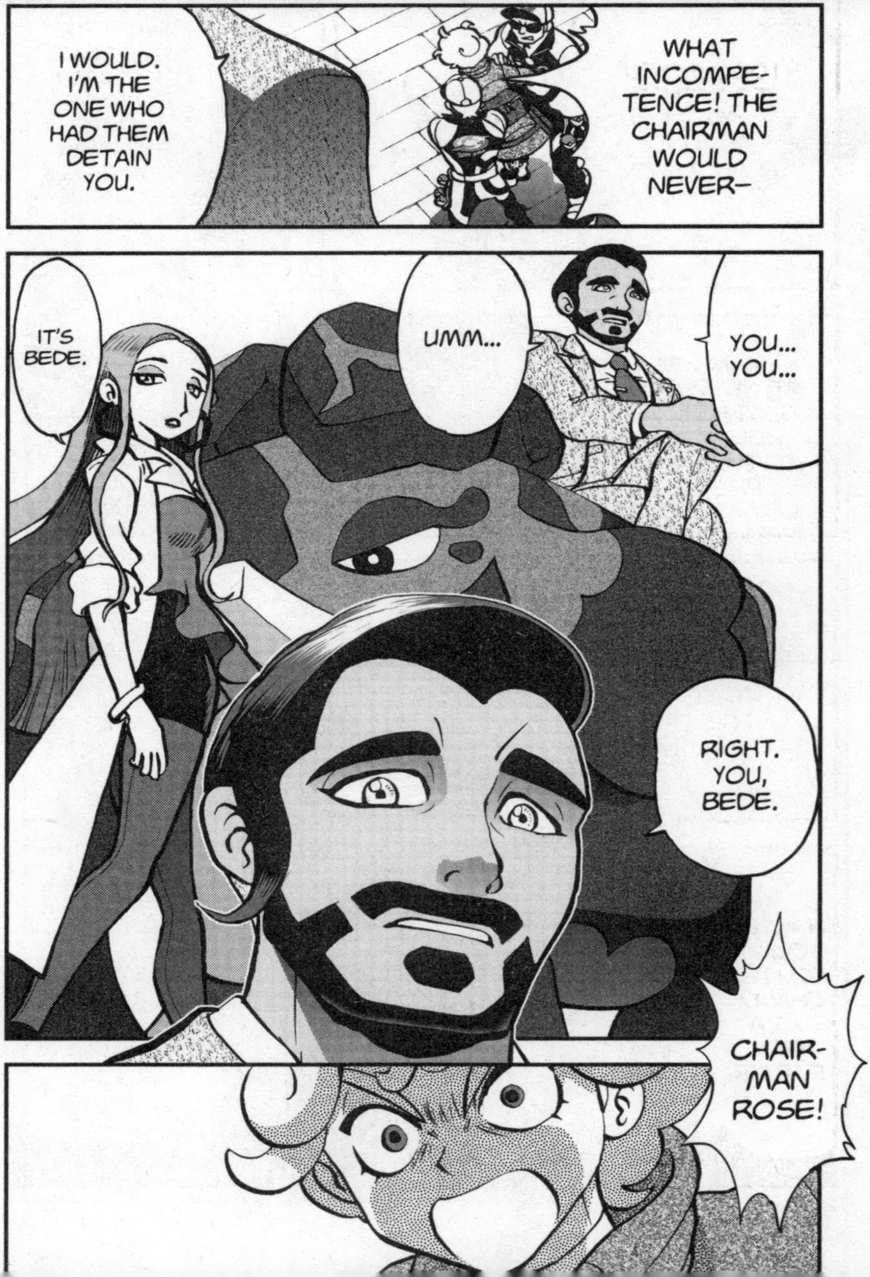
WHAT INCOMPETENCE! THE CHAIRMAN WOULD NEVER—
I WOULD. I'M THE ONE WHO HAD THEM DETAIN YOU.
YOU... YOU...
UMM...
IT'S BEDE.
RIGHT. YOU, BEDE.
CHAIRMAN ROSE!

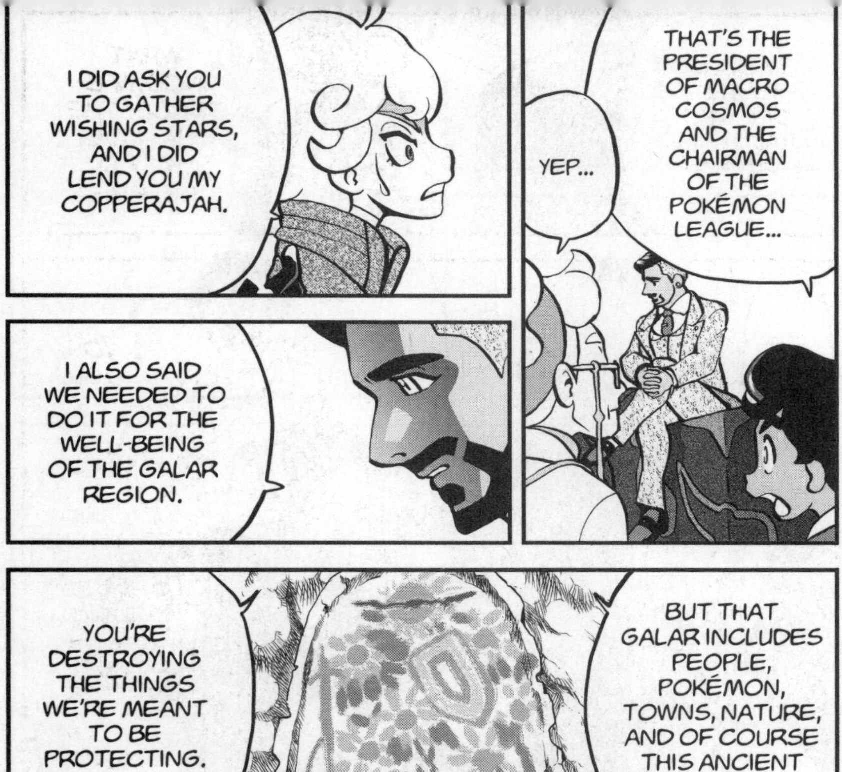

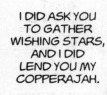

THAT'S THE PRESIDENT OF MACRO COSMOS AND THE CHAIRMAN OF THE POKÉMON LEAGUE...
YEP...
I DID ASK YOU TO GATHER WISHING STARS, AND I DID LEND YOU MY COPPERAJAH.
I ALSO SAID WE NEEDED TO DO IT FOR THE WELL-BEING OF THE GALAR REGION.
BUT THAT GALAR INCLUDES PEOPLE, POKÉMON, TOWNS, NATURE, AND OF COURSE THIS ANCIENT RELIC AS WELL.
YOU'RE DESTROYING THE THINGS WE'RE MEANT TO BE PROTECTING.
I SAW A LITTLE BIT OF MYSELF IN YOU WHEN YOU WERE A CHILD.
I CHOSE YOU AND SENT YOU TO THE TRAINERS' SCHOOL TO HONE YOUR SKILLS.
I WANTED TO GIVE YOU THE CHANCE AT A REAL FUTURE.

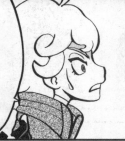

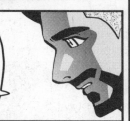

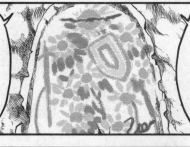

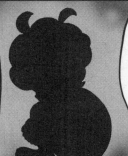

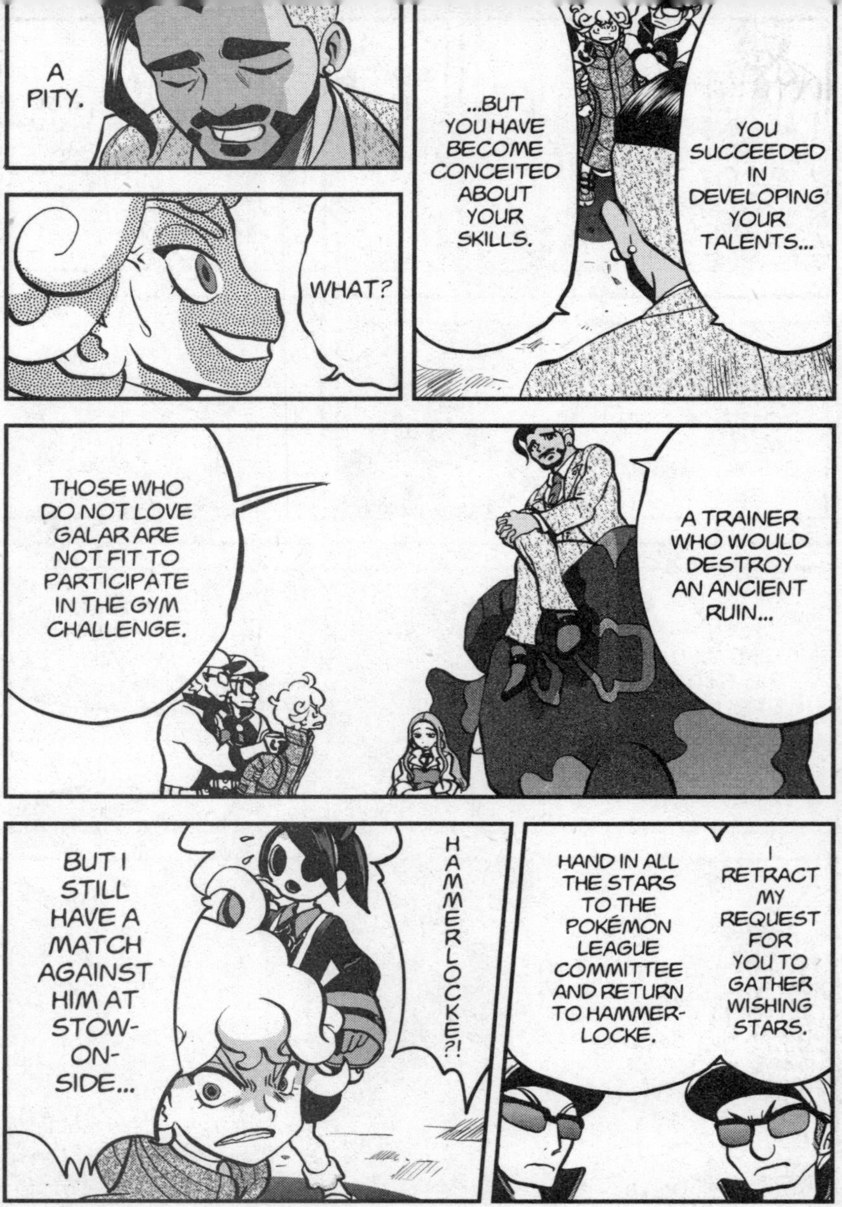
YOU SUCCEEDED IN DEVELOPING YOUR TALENTS...
...BUT YOU HAVE BECOME CONCEITED ABOUT YOUR SKILLS.
A PITY.
WHAT?
A TRAINER WHO WOULD DESTROY AN ANCIENT RUIN...
THOSE WHO DO NOT LOVE GALAR ARE NOT FIT TO PARTICIPATE IN THE GYM CHALLENGE.
I RETRACT MY REQUEST FOR YOU TO GATHER WISHING STARS.
HAND IN ALL THE STARS TO THE POKÉMON LEAGUE COMMITTEE AND RETURN TO HAMMER-LOCKE.
HAMMERLOCKE?!
BUT I STILL HAVE A MATCH AGAINST HIM AT STOW-ON-SIDE...

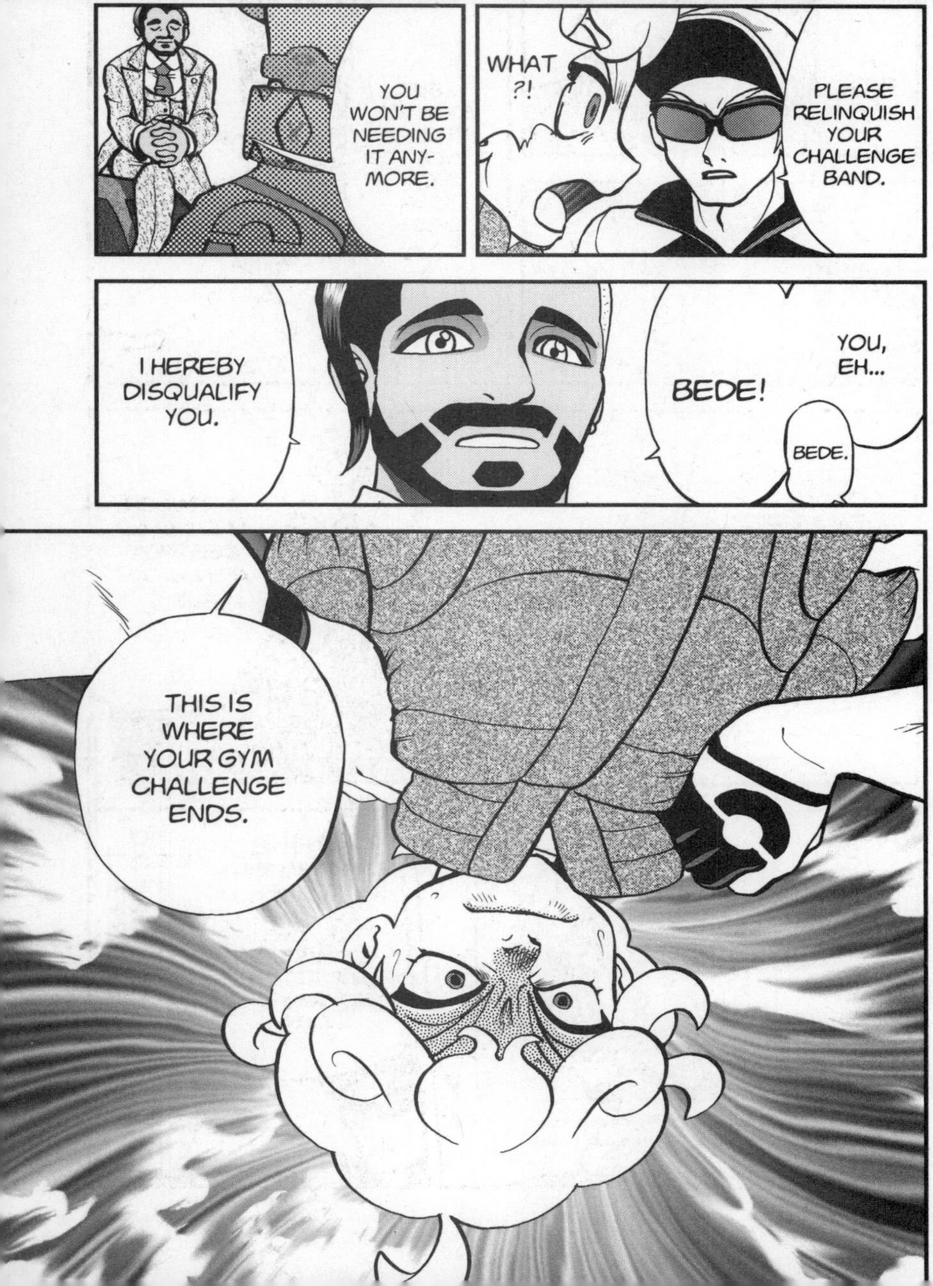
PLEASE RELINQUISH YOUR CHALLENGE BAND.
WHAT ?!
YOU WON'T BE NEEDING IT ANY-MORE.
YOU, EH... BEDE!
BEDE.
I HEREBY DISQUALIFY YOU.
THIS IS WHERE YOUR GYM CHALLENGE ENDS.

Geoglyph

▲ Is the geoglyph a record of the ancient people's fear?!

On the outskirts of Turffield lies this massive geoglyph. Sonia says it's depicting the Dynamax phenomenon!

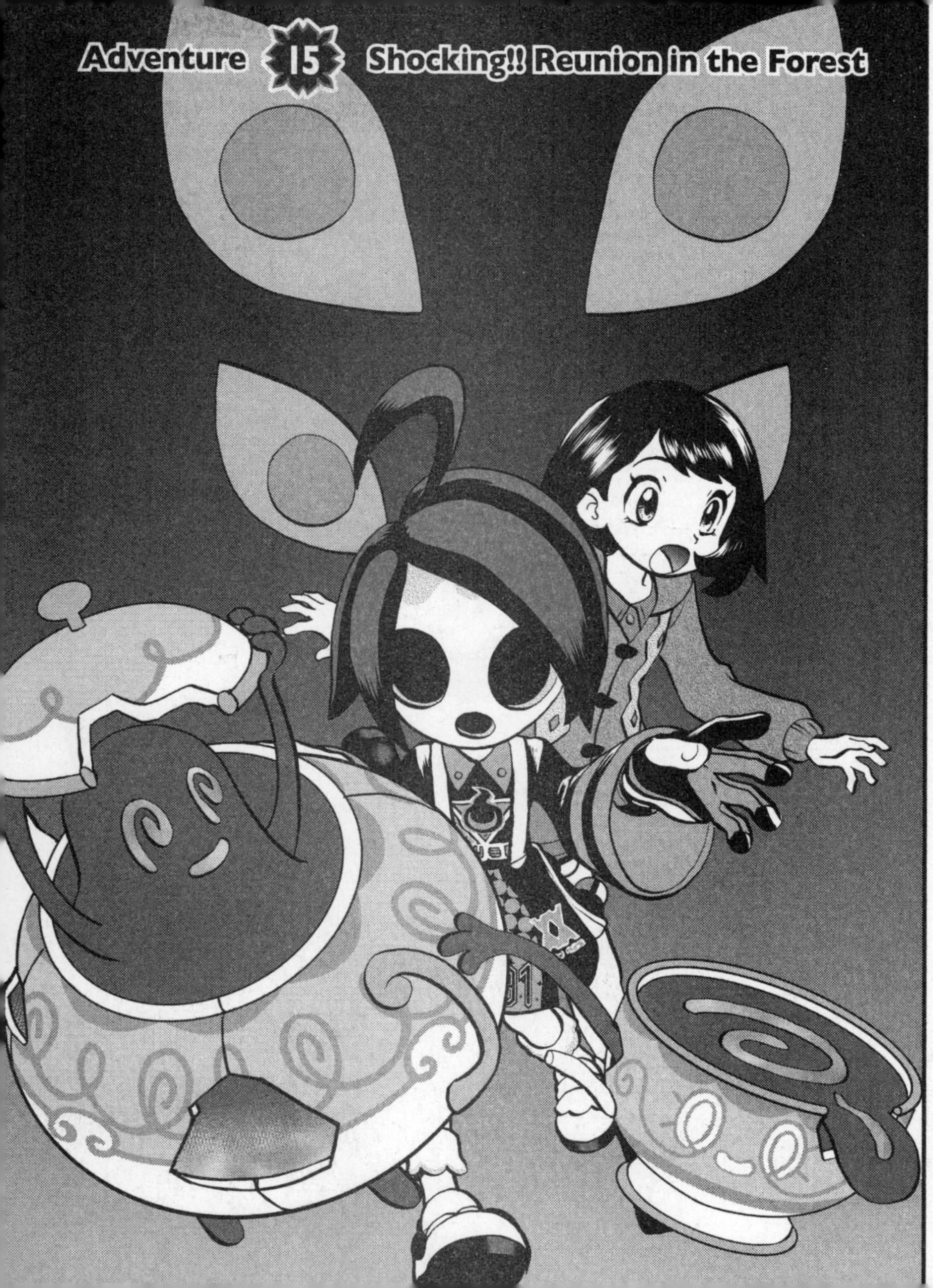
Adventure 15 Shocking!! Reunion in the Forest

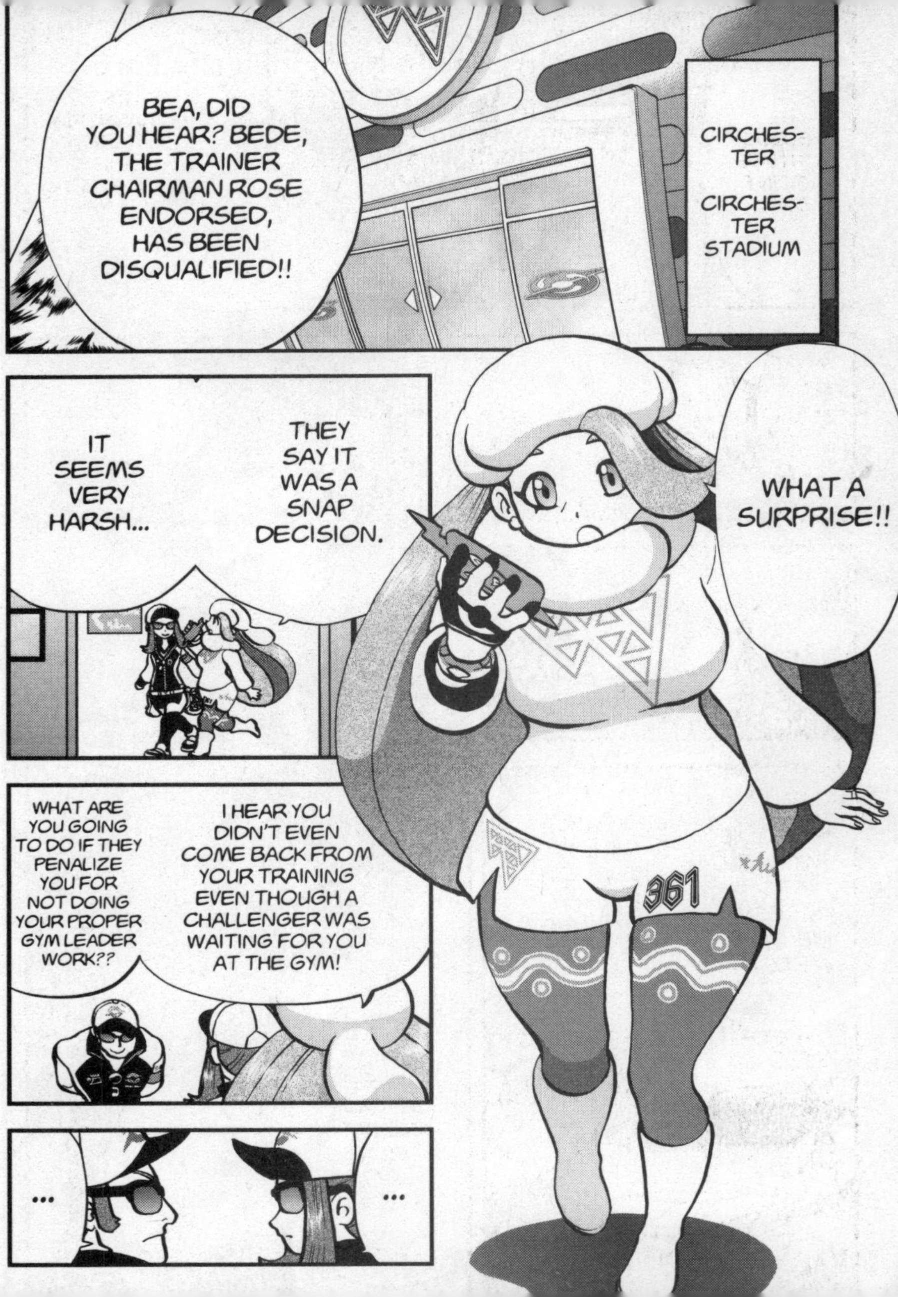
CIRCHES-
TER

CIRCHES-
TER
STADIUM
BEA, DID YOU HEAR? BEDE, THE TRAINER CHAIRMAN ROSE ENDORSED, HAS BEEN DISQUALIFIED!!
WHAT A SURPRISE!!
THEY SAY IT WAS A SNAP DECISION.
IT SEEMS VERY HARSH...
I HEAR YOU DIDN'T EVEN COME BACK FROM YOUR TRAINING EVEN THOUGH A CHALLENGER WAS WAITING FOR YOU AT THE GYM!
WHAT ARE YOU GOING TO DO IF THEY PENALIZE YOU FOR NOT DOING YOUR PROPER GYM LEADER WORK??
...
...

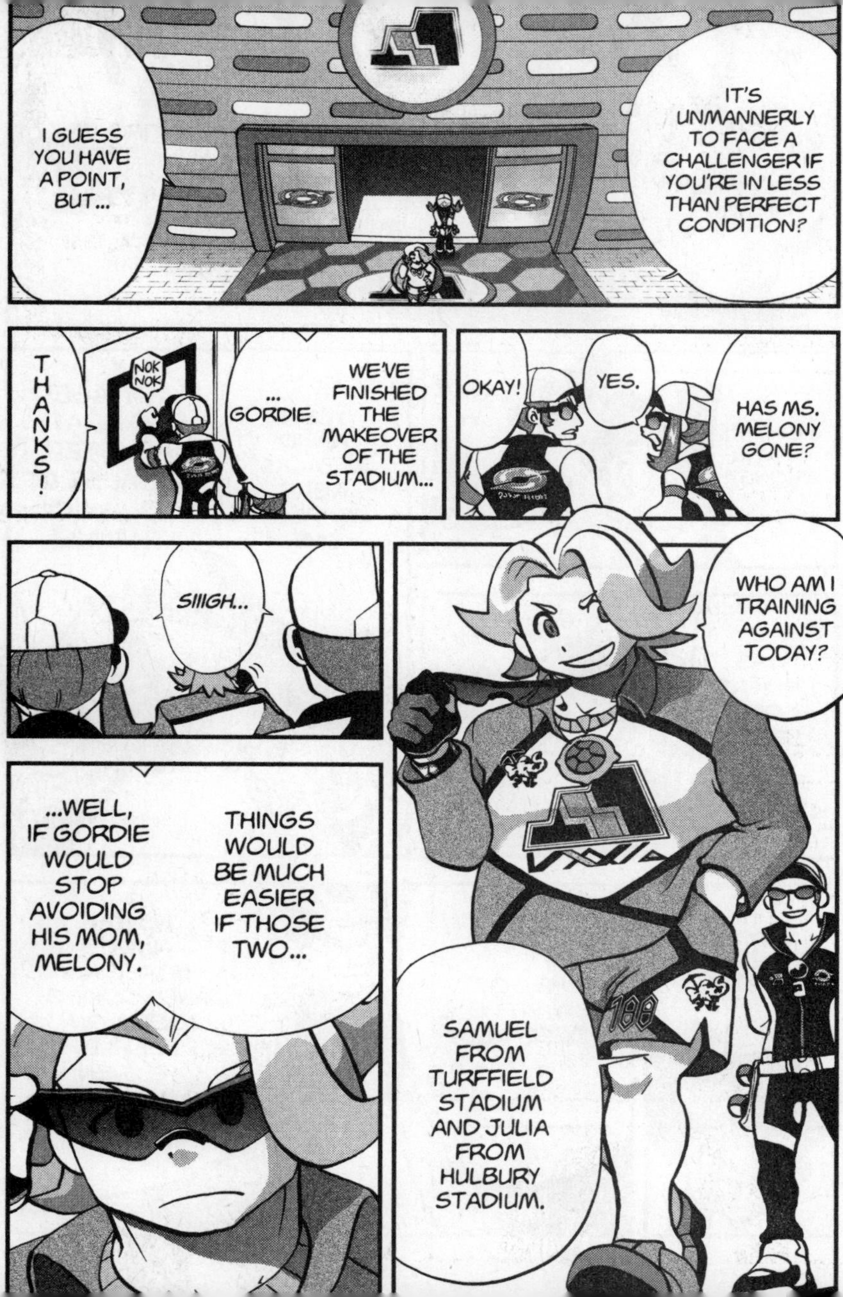
IT'S UNMANNERLY TO FACE A CHALLENGER IF YOU'RE IN LESS THAN PERFECT CONDITION?
I GUESS YOU HAVE A POINT, BUT...
HAS MS. MELONY GONE?
YES.
OKAY!
WE'VE FINISHED THE MAKEOVER OF THE STADIUM...
... GORDIE.
NOK NOK
THANKS!
WHO AM I TRAINING AGAINST TODAY?
SAMUEL FROM TURFFIELD STADIUM AND JULIA FROM HULBURY STADIUM.
SIIIGH...
THINGS WOULD BE MUCH EASIER IF THOSE TWO...
...WELL, IF GORDIE WOULD STOP AVOIDING HIS MOM, MELONY.

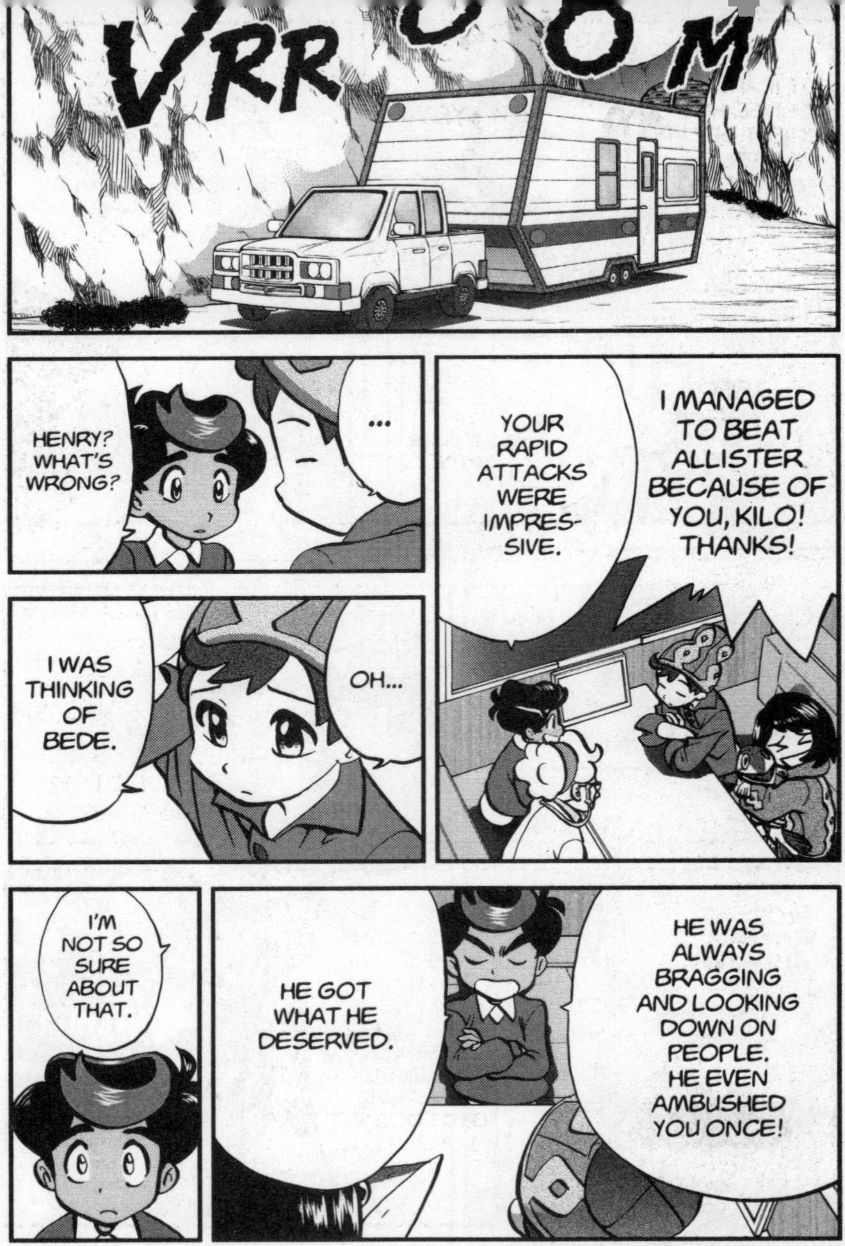
VRROOOM
I MANAGED TO BEAT ALLISTER BECAUSE OF YOU, KILO! THANKS!
YOUR RAPID ATTACKS WERE IMPRES-SIVE.
...
HENRY? WHAT'S WRONG?
OH...
I WAS THINKING OF BEDE.
HE WAS ALWAYS BRAGGING AND LOOKING DOWN ON PEOPLE. HE EVEN AMBUSHED YOU ONCE!
HE GOT WHAT HE DESERVED.
I'M NOT SO SURE ABOUT THAT.

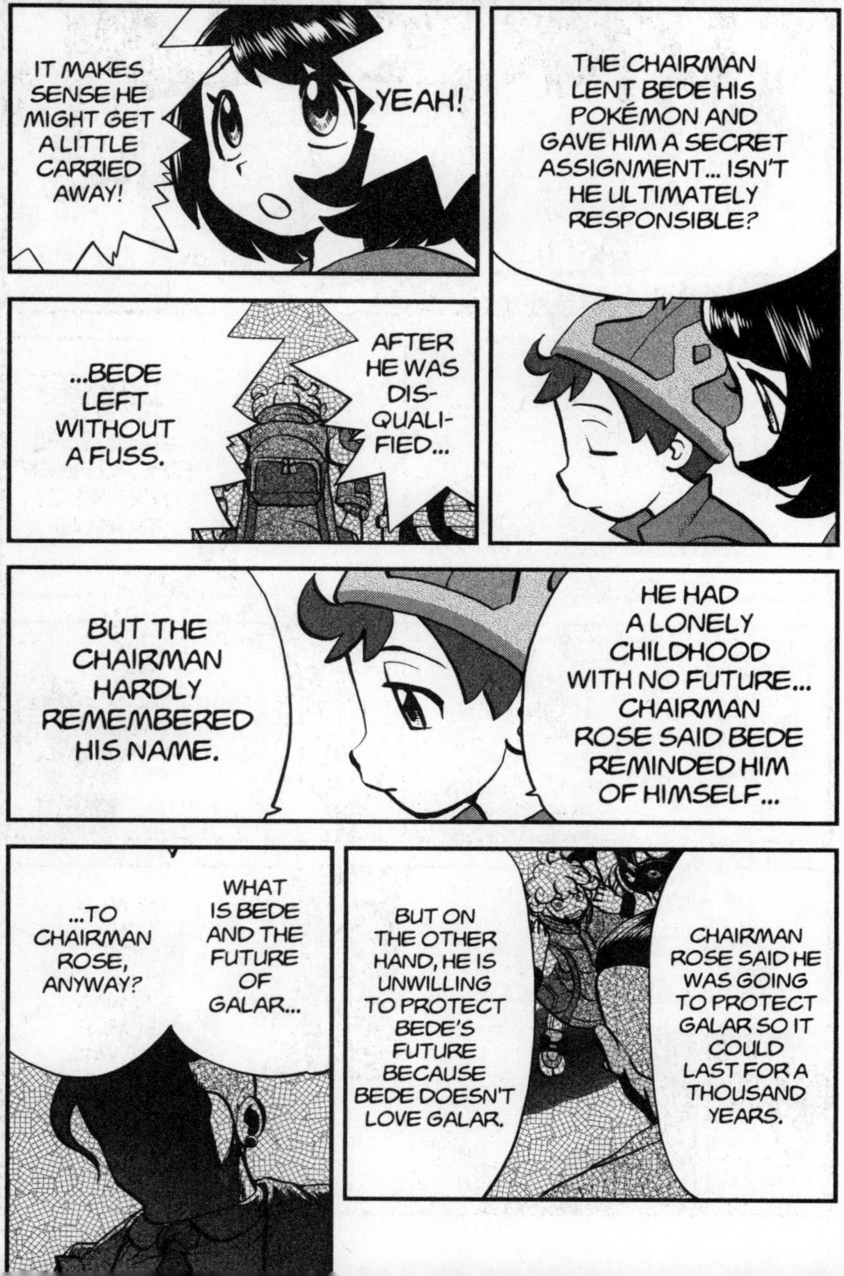
THE CHAIRMAN LENT BEDE HIS POKÉMON AND GAVE HIM A SECRET ASSIGNMENT... ISN'T HE ULTIMATELY RESPONSIBLE?
YEAH!
IT MAKES SENSE HE MIGHT GET A LITTLE CARRIED AWAY!
AFTER HE WAS DIS-QUALI-FIED...
...BEDE LEFT WITHOUT A FUSS.
HE HAD A LONELY CHILDHOOD WITH NO FUTURE... CHAIRMAN ROSE SAID BEDE REMINDED HIM OF HIMSELF...
BUT THE CHAIRMAN HARDLY REMEMBERED HIS NAME.
CHAIRMAN ROSE SAID HE WAS GOING TO PROTECT GALAR SO IT COULD LAST FOR A THOUSAND YEARS.
BUT ON THE OTHER HAND, HE IS UNWILLING TO PROTECT BEDE'S FUTURE BECAUSE BEDE DOESN'T LOVE GALAR.
WHAT IS BEDE AND THE FUTURE OF GALAR...
...TO CHAIRMAN ROSE, ANYWAY?

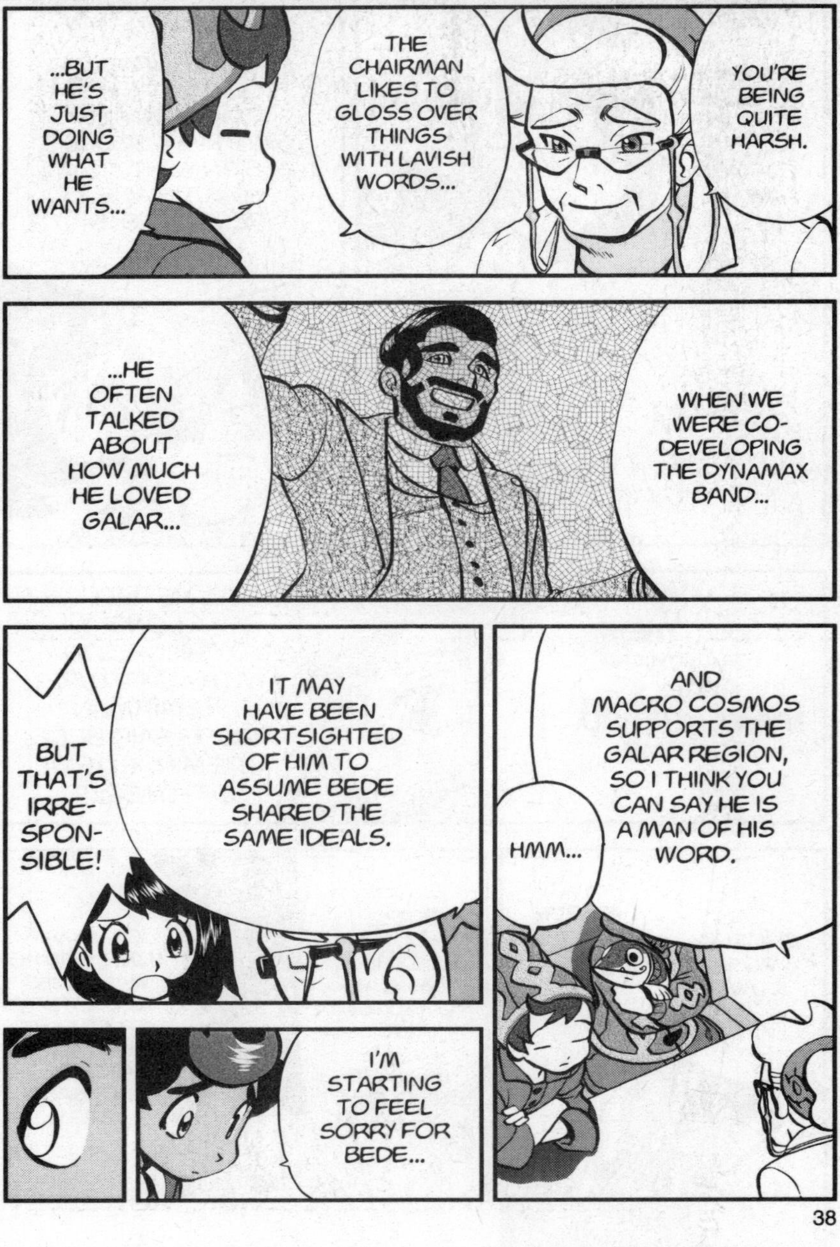
YOU'RE BEING QUITE HARSH.
THE CHAIRMAN LIKES TO GLOSS OVER THINGS WITH LAVISH WORDS...
...BUT HE'S JUST DOING WHAT HE WANTS...
WHEN WE WERE CO-DEVELOPING THE DYNAMAX BAND...
...HE OFTEN TALKED ABOUT HOW MUCH HE LOVED GALAR...
AND MACRO COSMOS SUPPORTS THE GALAR REGION, SO I THINK YOU CAN SAY HE IS A MAN OF HIS WORD.
HMM...
IT MAY HAVE BEEN SHORTSIGHTED OF HIM TO ASSUME BEDE SHARED THE SAME IDEALS.
BUT THAT'S IRRE-SPON-SIBLE!
I'M STARTING TO FEEL SORRY FOR BEDE...

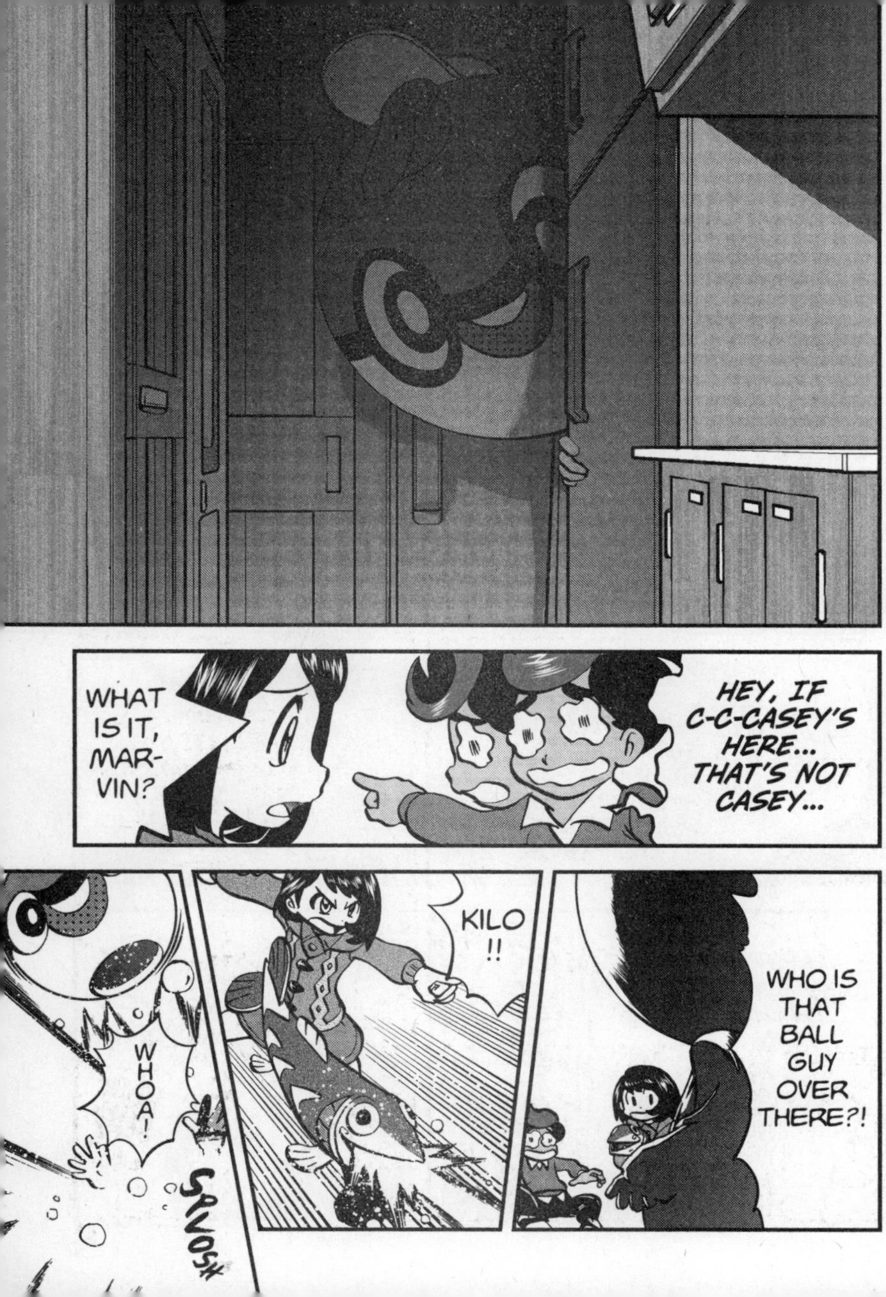
HEY, IF C-C-CASEY'S HERE... THAT'S NOT CASEY...
WHAT IS IT, MAR-VIN?
WHO IS THAT BALL GUY OVER THERE?!
KILO !!
WHOA!
SPVOSH

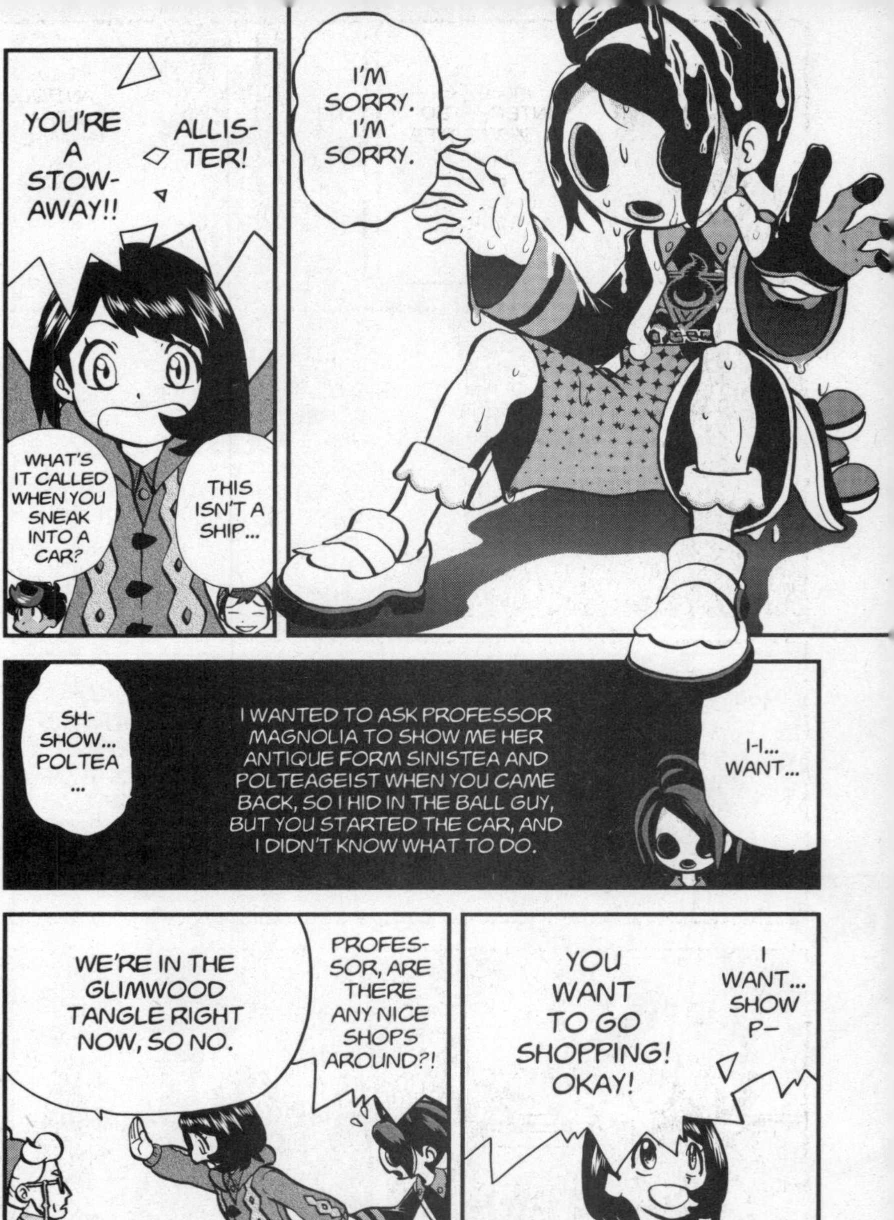
I'M SORRY. I'M SORRY.
ALLIS-TER!
YOU'RE A STOW-AWAY!!
THIS ISN'T A SHIP...
WHAT'S IT CALLED WHEN YOU SNEAK INTO A CAR?
I-I... WANT...
I WANTED TO ASK PROFESSOR MAGNOLIA TO SHOW ME HER ANTIQUE FORM SINISTEA AND POLTEAGEIST WHEN YOU CAME BACK, SO I HID IN THE BALL GUY, BUT YOU STARTED THE CAR, AND I DIDN'T KNOW WHAT TO DO.
SH-SHOW... POLTEA ...
I WANT... SHOW P—
YOU WANT TO GO SHOPPING! OKAY!
PROFES-SOR, ARE THERE ANY NICE SHOPS AROUND?!
WE'RE IN THE GLIMWOOD TANGLE RIGHT NOW, SO NO.

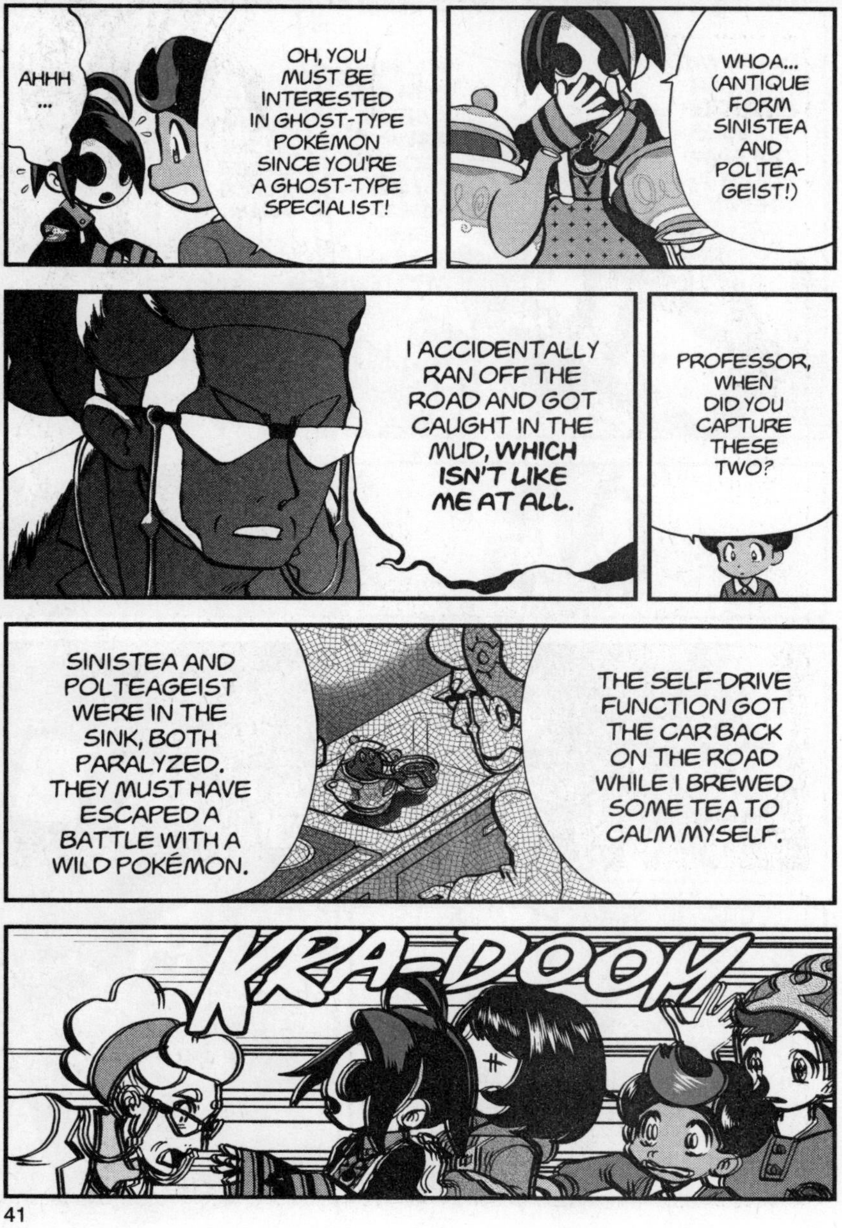
WHOA... (ANTIQUE FORM SINISTEA AND POLTEAGEIST!)
OH, YOU MUST BE INTERESTED IN GHOST-TYPE POKÉMON SINCE YOU'RE A GHOST-TYPE SPECIALIST!
AHHH ...
PROFESSOR, WHEN DID YOU CAPTURE THESE TWO?
I ACCIDENTALLY RAN OFF THE ROAD AND GOT CAUGHT IN THE MUD, **WHICH ISN'T LIKE ME AT ALL.**
THE SELF-DRIVE FUNCTION GOT THE CAR BACK ON THE ROAD WHILE I BREWED SOME TEA TO CALM MYSELF.
SINISTEA AND POLTEAGEIST WERE IN THE SINK, BOTH PARALYZED. THEY MUST HAVE ESCAPED A BATTLE WITH A WILD POKÉMON.
KRA-DOOM

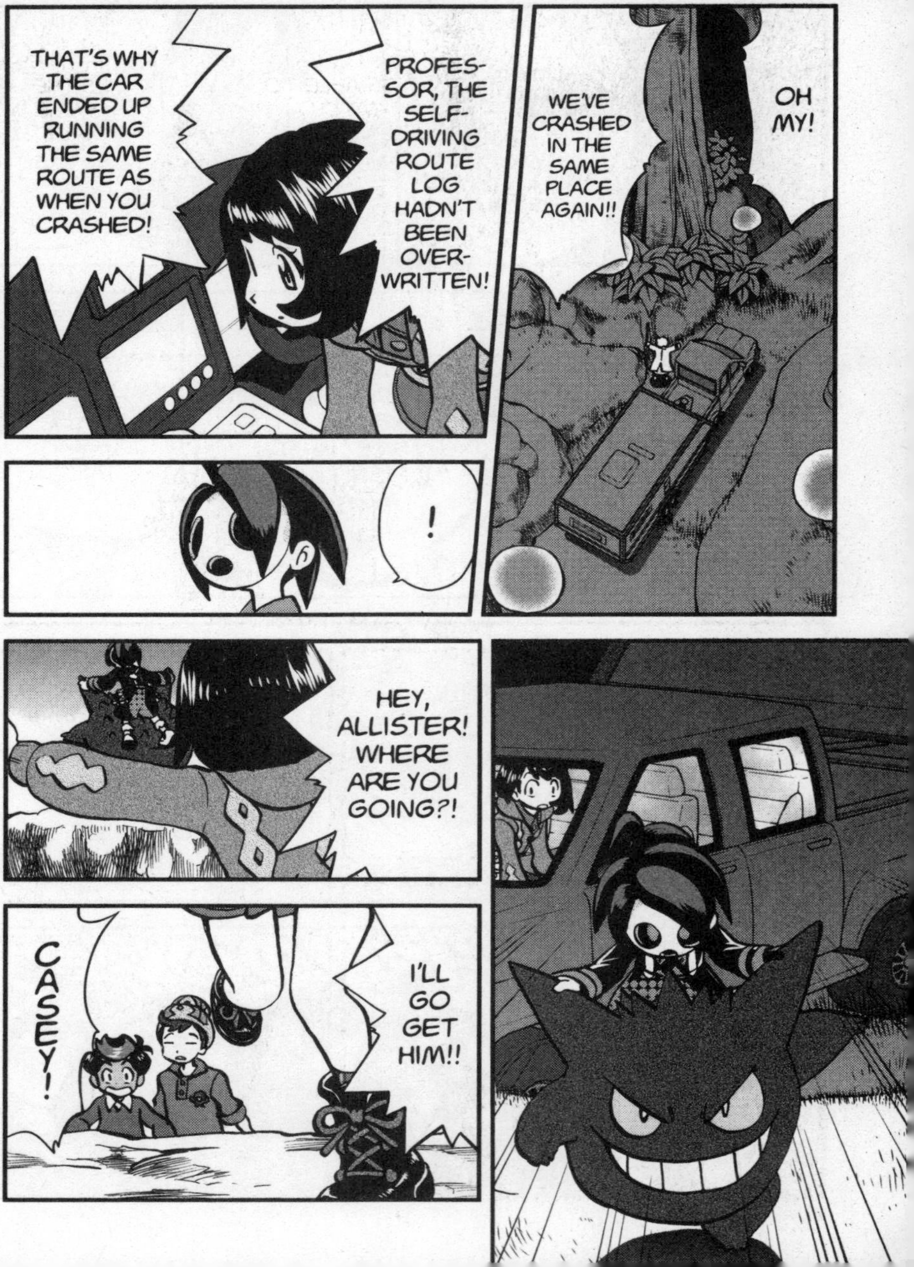
OH MY!
WE'VE CRASHED IN THE SAME PLACE AGAIN!!
PROFESSOR, THE SELF-DRIVING ROUTE LOG HADN'T BEEN OVERWRITTEN!
THAT'S WHY THE CAR ENDED UP RUNNING THE SAME ROUTE AS WHEN YOU CRASHED!
!
HEY, ALLISTER! WHERE ARE YOU GOING?!
I'LL GO GET HIM!!
CASEY!

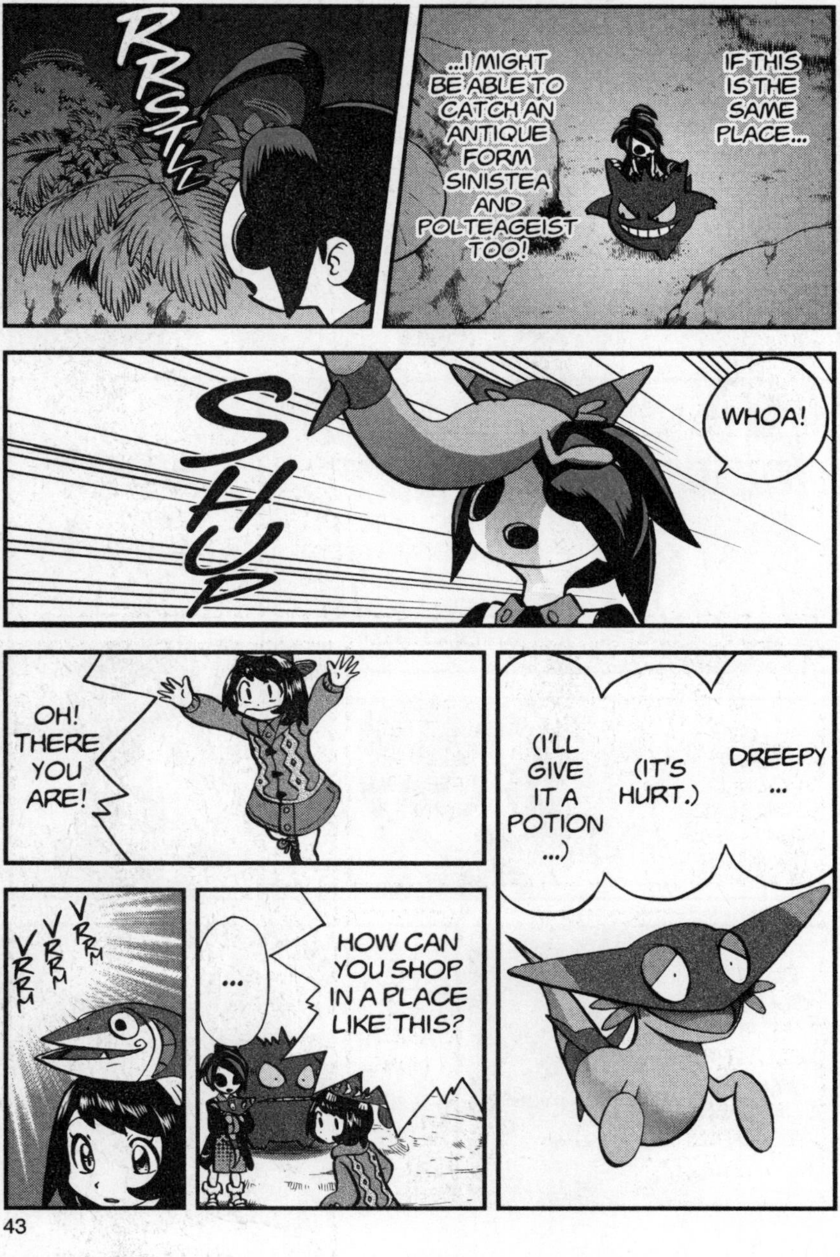
IF THIS IS THE SAME PLACE...
...I MIGHT BE ABLE TO CATCH AN ANTIQUE FORM SINISTEA AND POLTEAGEIST TOO!
RRSTLL
WHOA!
SHUP
DREEPY...
(IT'S HURT.)
(I'LL GIVE IT A POTION...)
OH! THERE YOU ARE!
HOW CAN YOU SHOP IN A PLACE LIKE THIS?
...
VRRM VRRM VRRM

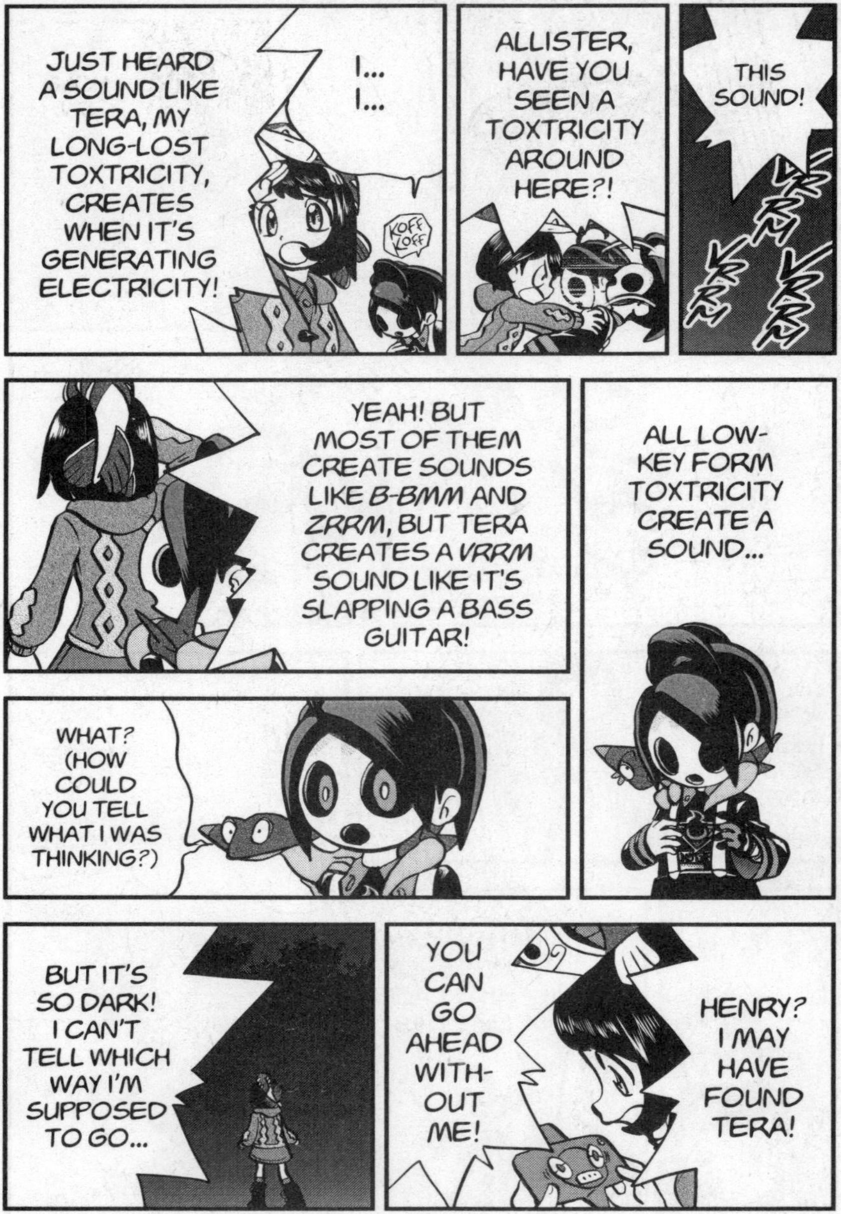
THIS SOUND!
VRRM VRRM VRRM
ALLISTER, HAVE YOU SEEN A TOXTRICITY AROUND HERE?!
I... I...
JUST HEARD A SOUND LIKE TERA, MY LONG-LOST TOXTRICITY, CREATES WHEN IT'S GENERATING ELECTRICITY!
KOFF KOFF
ALL LOW-KEY FORM TOXTRICITY CREATE A SOUND...
YEAH! BUT MOST OF THEM CREATE SOUNDS LIKE B-BMM AND ZRRM, BUT TERA CREATES A VRRM SOUND LIKE IT'S SLAPPING A BASS GUITAR!
WHAT? (HOW COULD YOU TELL WHAT I WAS THINKING?)
HENRY? I MAY HAVE FOUND TERA!
YOU CAN GO AHEAD WITH-OUT ME!
BUT IT'S SO DARK! I CAN'T TELL WHICH WAY I'M SUPPOSED TO GO...

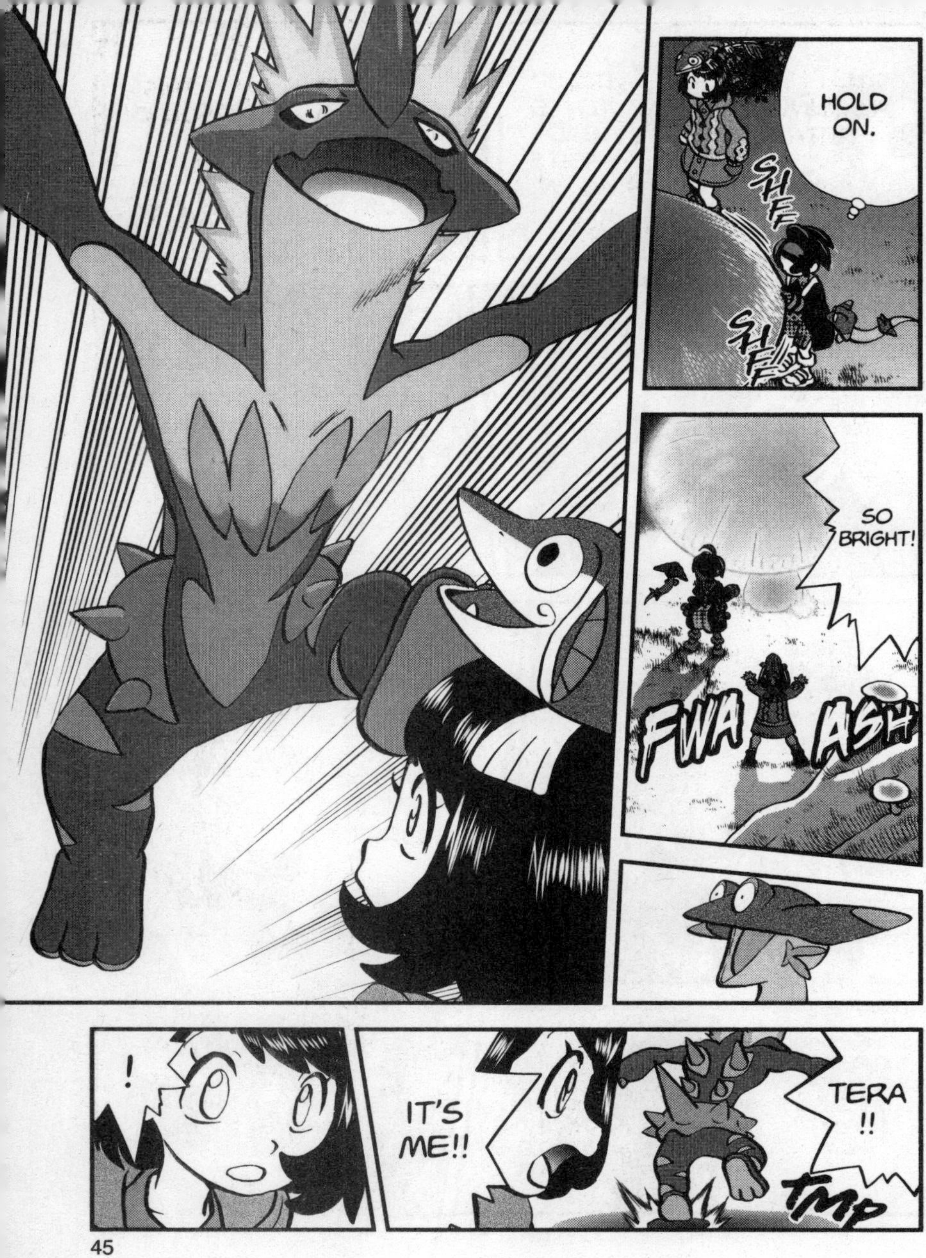
HOLD ON.
SHFF
SHFF
SO BRIGHT!
FWAASH
TERA !!
IT'S ME!!
TMP
!

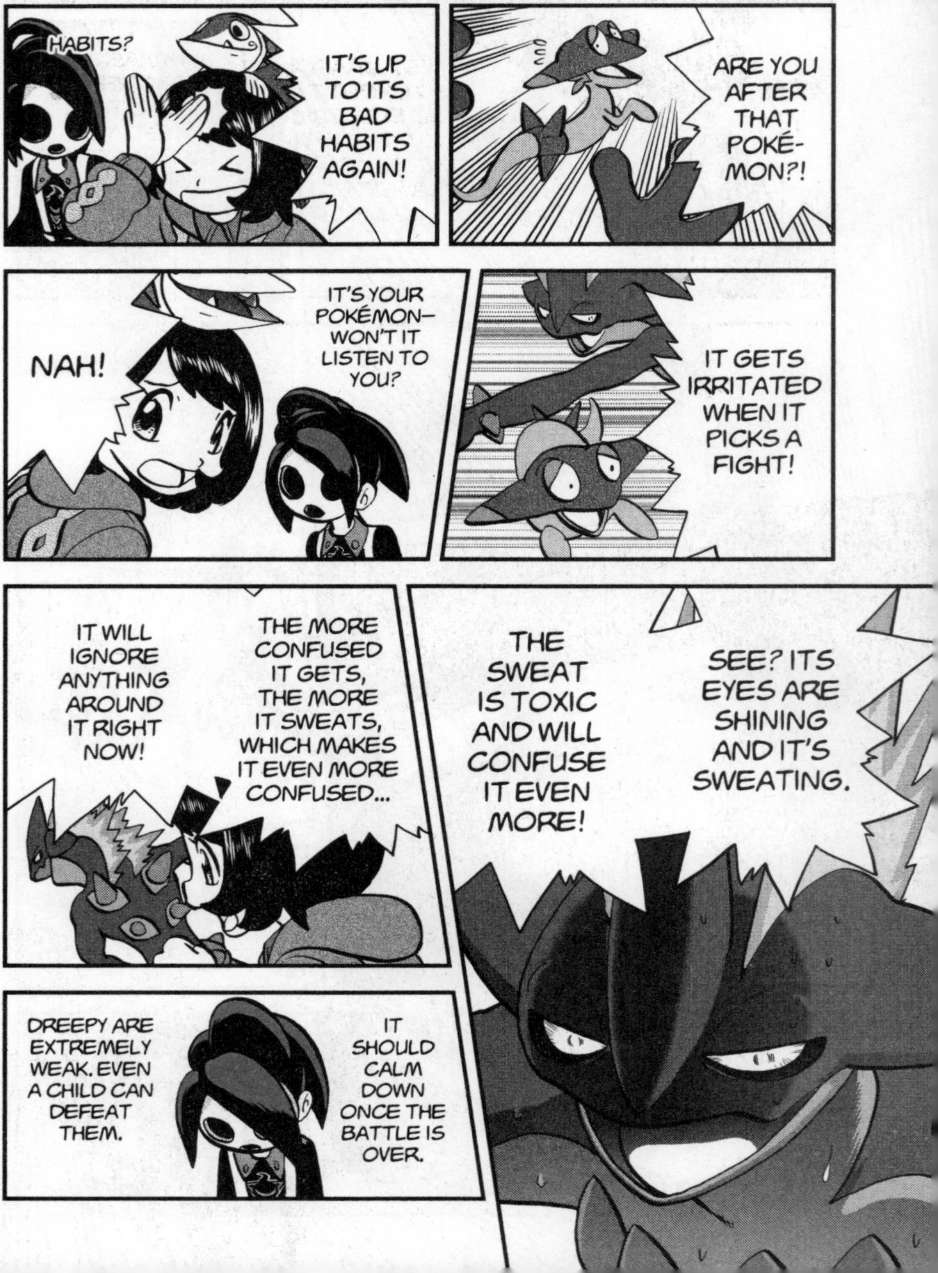
ARE YOU AFTER THAT POKÉMON?!
IT'S UP TO ITS BAD HABITS AGAIN!
HABITS?
IT GETS IRRITATED WHEN IT PICKS A FIGHT!
IT'S YOUR POKÉMON—WON'T IT LISTEN TO YOU?
NAH!
SEE? ITS EYES ARE SHINING AND IT'S SWEATING.
THE SWEAT IS TOXIC AND WILL CONFUSE IT EVEN MORE!
THE MORE CONFUSED IT GETS, THE MORE IT SWEATS, WHICH MAKES IT EVEN MORE CONFUSED...
IT WILL IGNORE ANYTHING AROUND IT RIGHT NOW!
IT SHOULD CALM DOWN ONCE THE BATTLE IS OVER.
DREEPY ARE EXTREMELY WEAK. EVEN A CHILD CAN DEFEAT THEM.

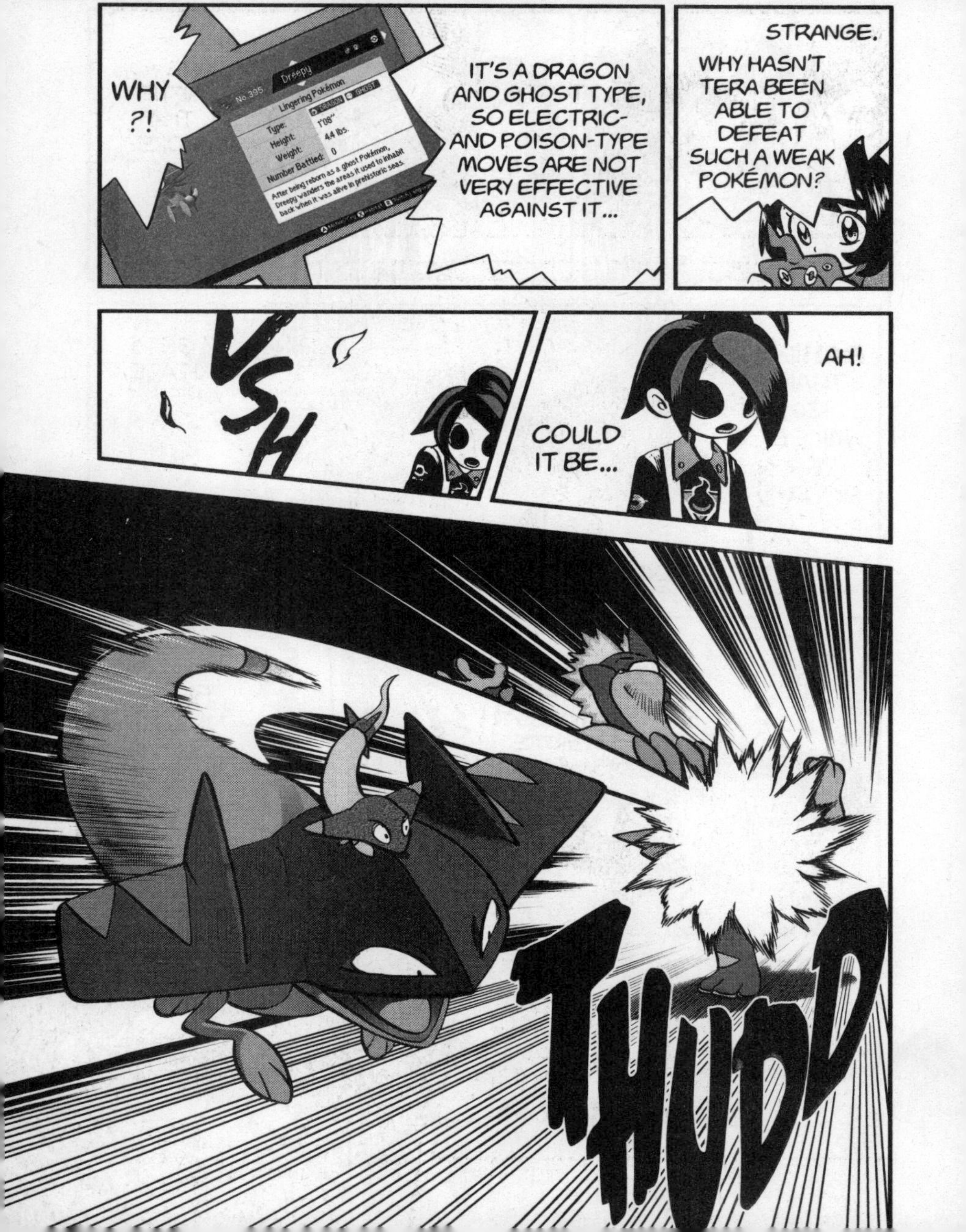
STRANGE.
WHY HASN'T TERA BEEN ABLE TO DEFEAT SUCH A WEAK POKÉMON?
IT'S A DRAGON AND GHOST TYPE, SO ELECTRIC- AND POISON-TYPE MOVES ARE NOT VERY EFFECTIVE AGAINST IT...
WHY ?!
No.395 Dreepy
Lingering Pokémon
Type: DRAGON GHOST
Height: 1'08"
Weight: 4.4 lbs.
Number Battled: 0
After being reborn as a ghost Pokémon, Dreepy wanders the areas it used to inhabit back when it was alive in prehistoric seas.
AH!
COULD IT BE...
VSH
THUDD

WHA-AAT?!

(ITS CARE-TAKER) DRAKLOAK (IS AROUND TOO)!

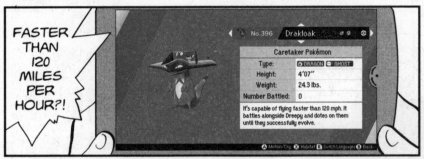

FASTER THAN 120 MILES PER HOUR?!

No.396 Drakloak

Caretaker Pokémon

Type:	DRAGON GHOST
Height:	4'07"
Weight:	24.3 lbs.
Number Battled:	0

It's capable of flying faster than 120 mph. It battles alongside Dreepy and dotes on them until they successfully evolve.

A Motion/Cry X Habitat R Switch Languages B Back

IT'S TOO EXCITED TO KEEP UP WITH ITS OPPONENT'S SPEED! WHAT SHOULD I DO?!

GRRR

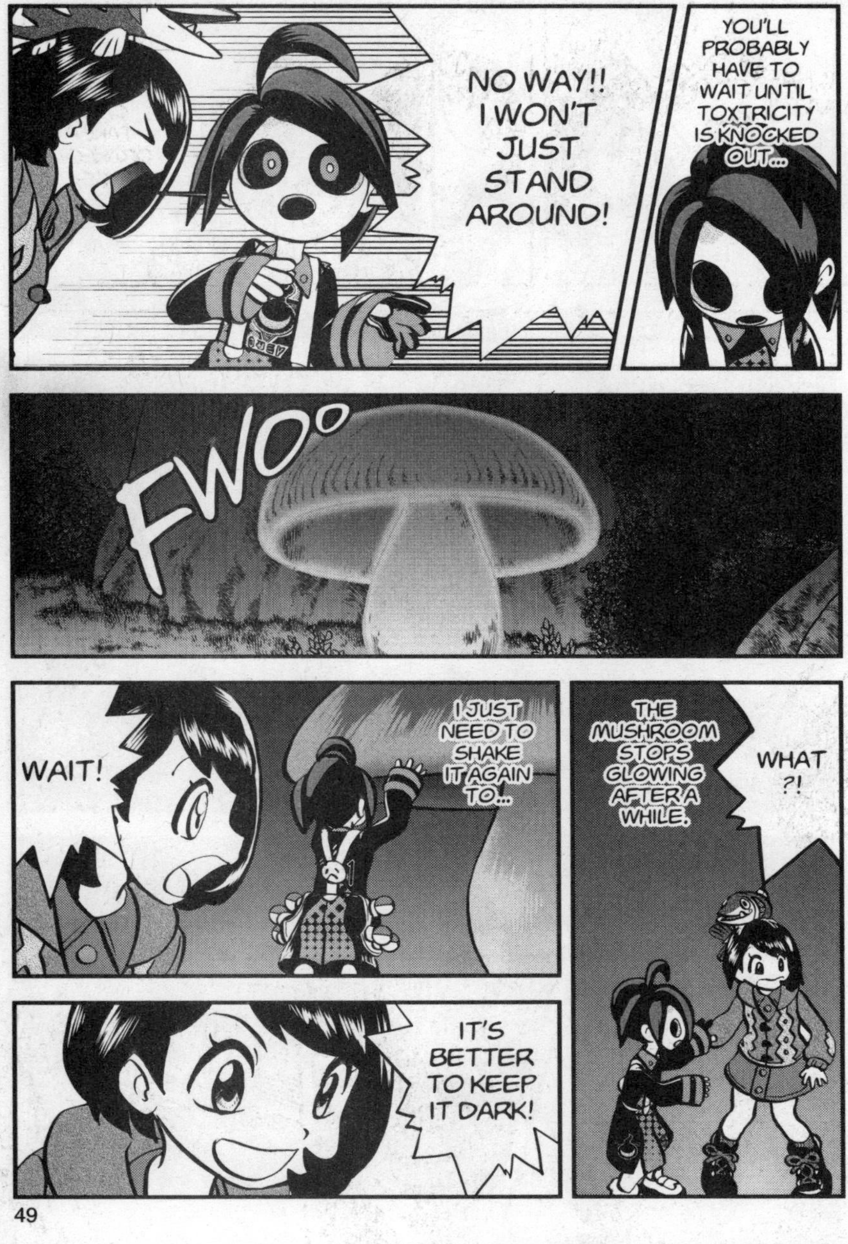
YOU'LL PROBABLY HAVE TO WAIT UNTIL TOXTRICITY IS KNOCKED OUT...
NO WAY!! I WON'T JUST STAND AROUND!
FWOo
WHAT ?!
THE MUSHROOM STOPS GLOWING AFTER A WHILE.
I JUST NEED TO SHAKE IT AGAIN TO...
WAIT!
IT'S BETTER TO KEEP IT DARK!

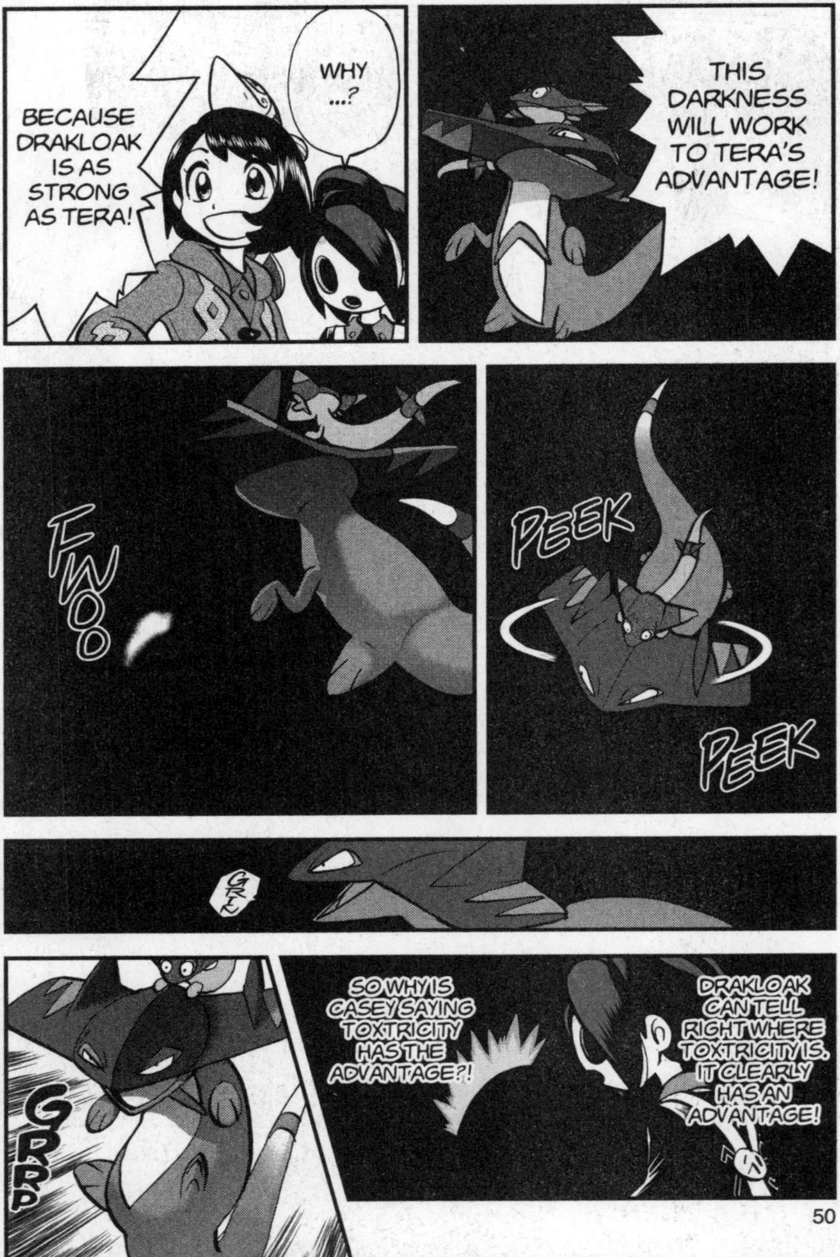
THIS DARKNESS WILL WORK TO TERA'S ADVANTAGE!
WHY ...?
BECAUSE DRAKLOAK IS AS STRONG AS TERA!
PEEK
PEEK
FWOO
GRIN
DRAKLOAK CAN TELL RIGHT WHERE TOXTRICITY IS. IT CLEARLY HAS AN ADVANTAGE!
SO WHY IS CASEY SAYING TOXTRICITY HAS THE ADVANTAGE?!
GRRRP

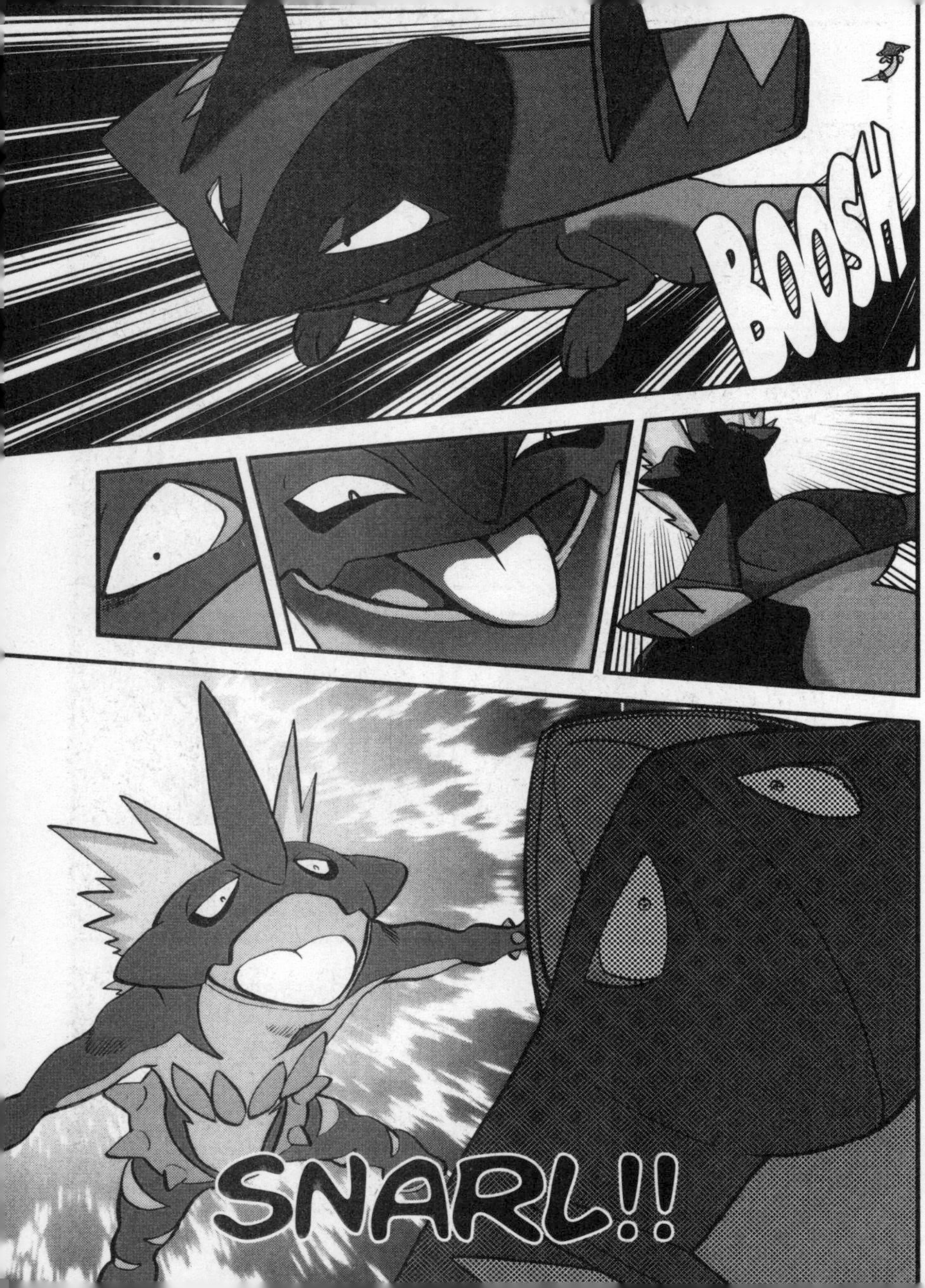
BOOSH
SNARL!!

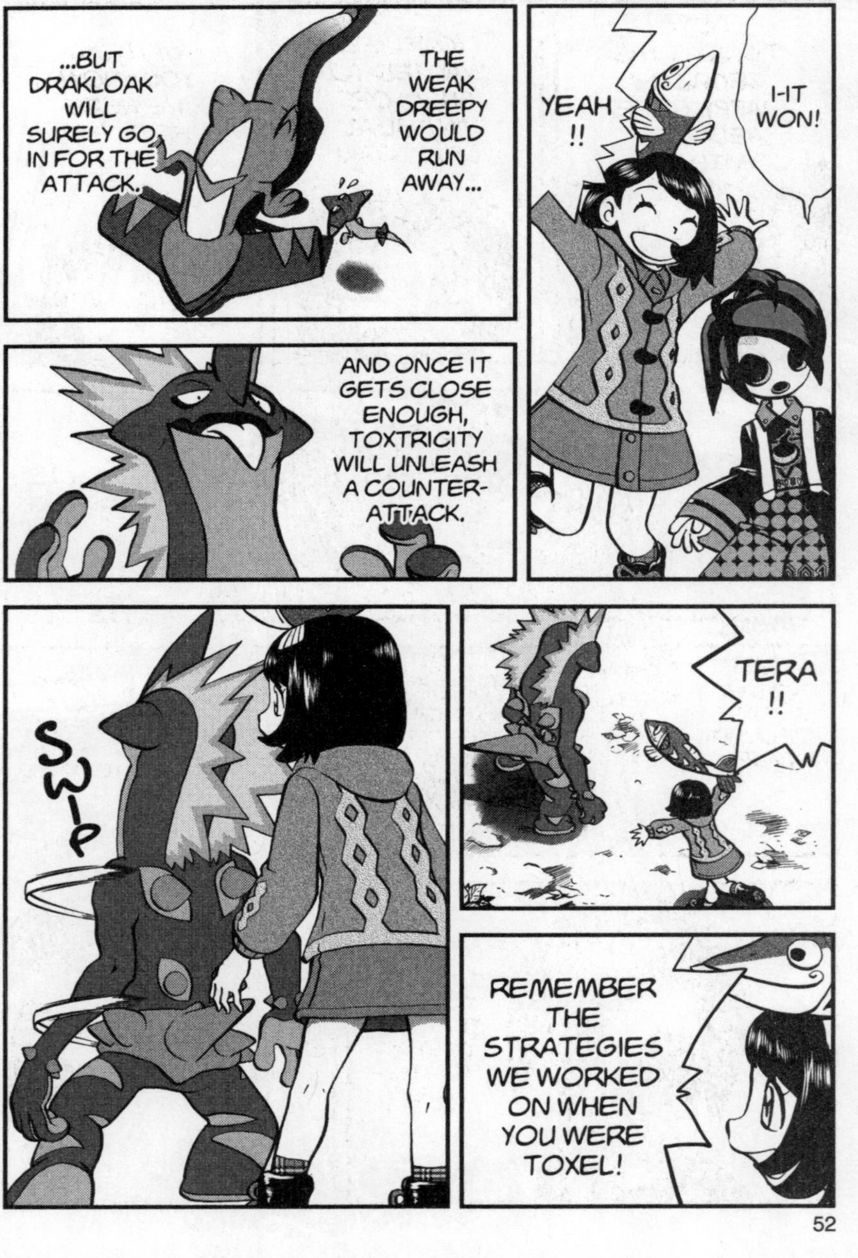
I-IT WON!
YEAH!!
THE WEAK DREEPY WOULD RUN AWAY...
...BUT DRAKLOAK WILL SURELY GO IN FOR THE ATTACK.
AND ONCE IT GETS CLOSE ENOUGH, TOXTRICITY WILL UNLEASH A COUNTER-ATTACK.
TERA!!
REMEMBER THE STRATEGIES WE WORKED ON WHEN YOU WERE TOXEL!
SWIP

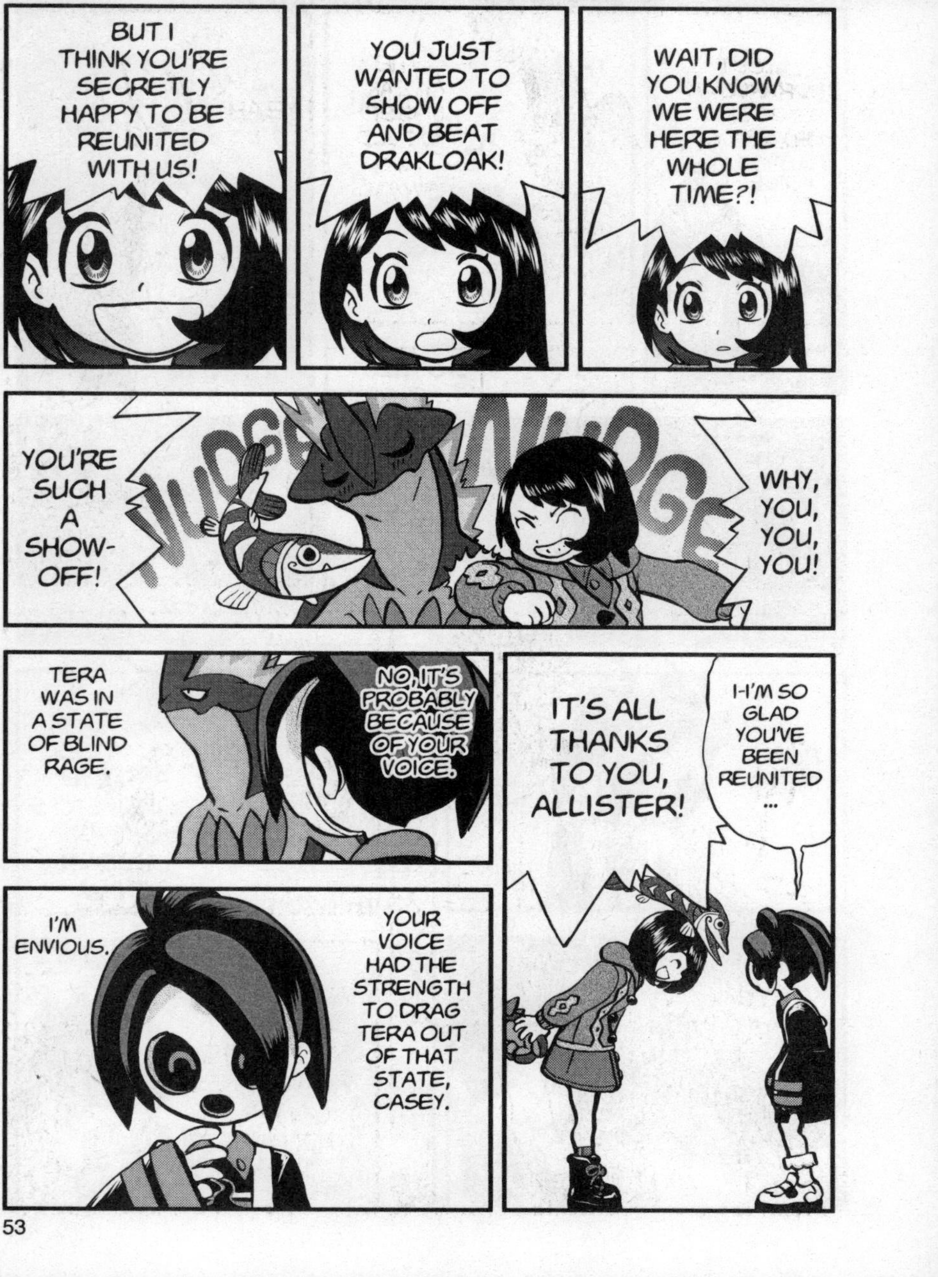
WAIT, DID YOU KNOW WE WERE HERE THE WHOLE TIME?!
YOU JUST WANTED TO SHOW OFF AND BEAT DRAKLOAK!
BUT I THINK YOU'RE SECRETLY HAPPY TO BE REUNITED WITH US!
WHY, YOU, YOU, YOU!
NUDGE NUDGE
YOU'RE SUCH A SHOW-OFF!
I-I'M SO GLAD YOU'VE BEEN REUNITED ...
IT'S ALL THANKS TO YOU, ALLISTER!
NO, IT'S PROBABLY BECAUSE OF YOUR VOICE.
TERA WAS IN A STATE OF BLIND RAGE.
YOUR VOICE HAD THE STRENGTH TO DRAG TERA OUT OF THAT STATE, CASEY.
I'M ENVIOUS.

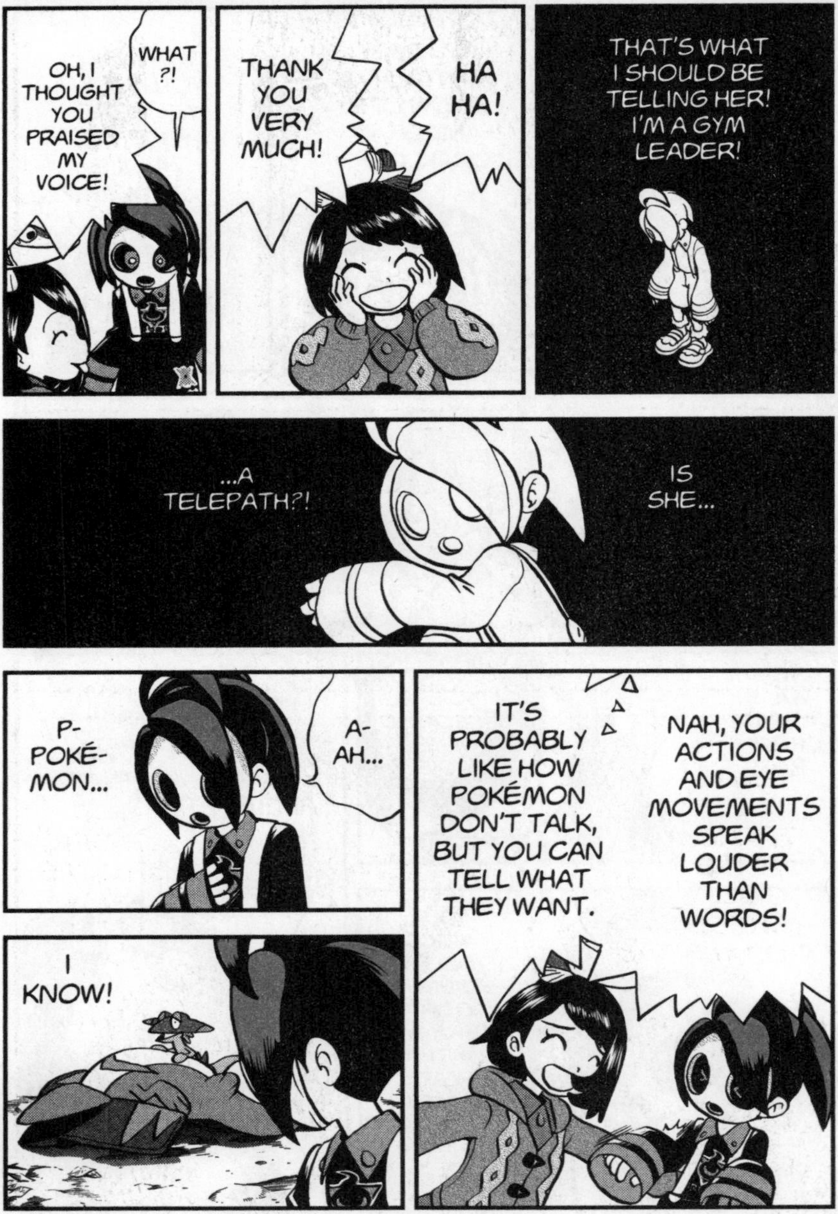
THAT'S WHAT I SHOULD BE TELLING HER! I'M A GYM LEADER!
HA HA!
THANK YOU VERY MUCH!
WHAT?!
OH, I THOUGHT YOU PRAISED MY VOICE!
IS SHE...
...A TELEPATH?!
NAH, YOUR ACTIONS AND EYE MOVEMENTS SPEAK LOUDER THAN WORDS!
IT'S PROBABLY LIKE HOW POKÉMON DON'T TALK, BUT YOU CAN TELL WHAT THEY WANT.
A-AH...
P-POKÉMON...
I KNOW!

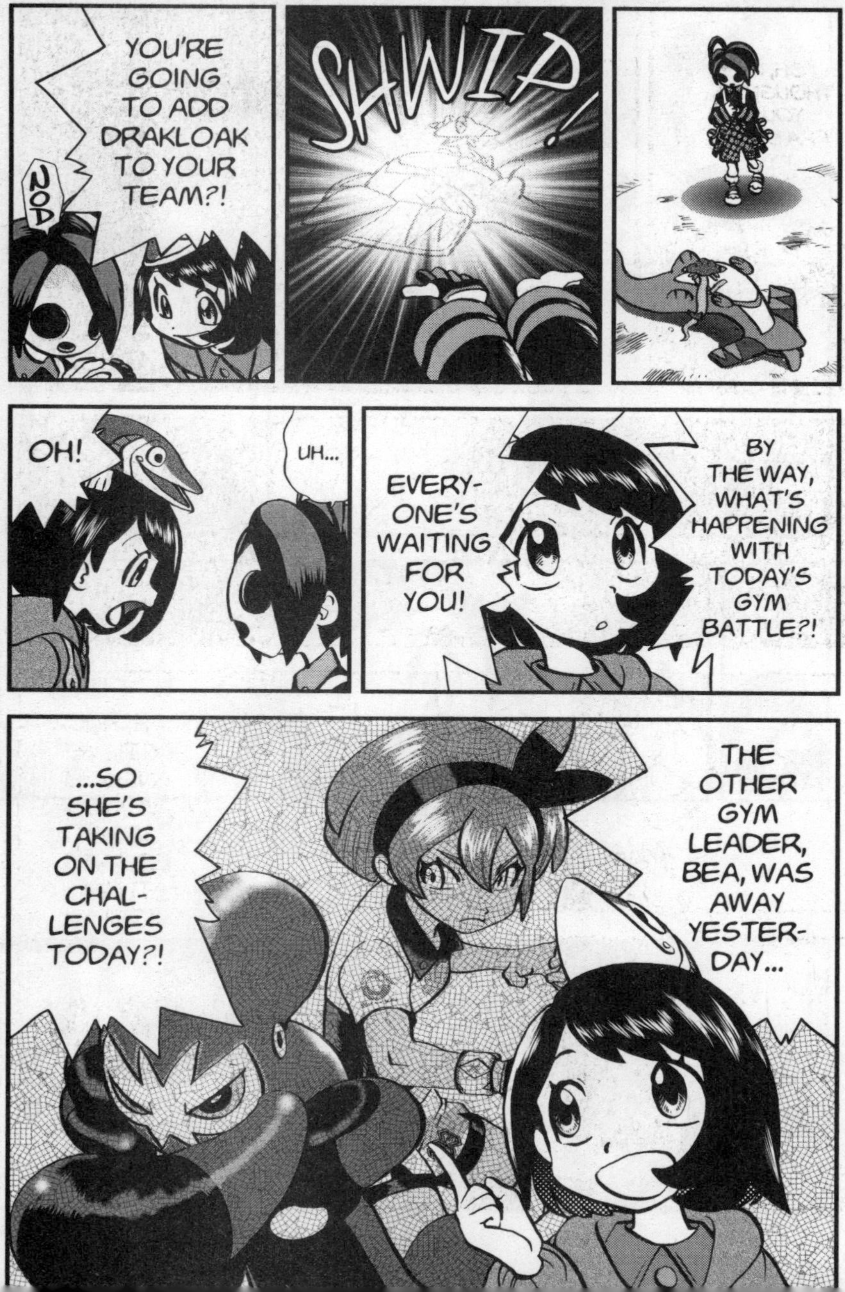
SHWIP!
YOU'RE GOING TO ADD DRAKLOAK TO YOUR TEAM?!
NOD
BY THE WAY, WHAT'S HAPPENING WITH TODAY'S GYM BATTLE?!
EVERY-ONE'S WAITING FOR YOU!
UH...
OH!
THE OTHER GYM LEADER, BEA, WAS AWAY YESTER-DAY...
...SO SHE'S TAKING ON THE CHAL-LENGES TODAY?!

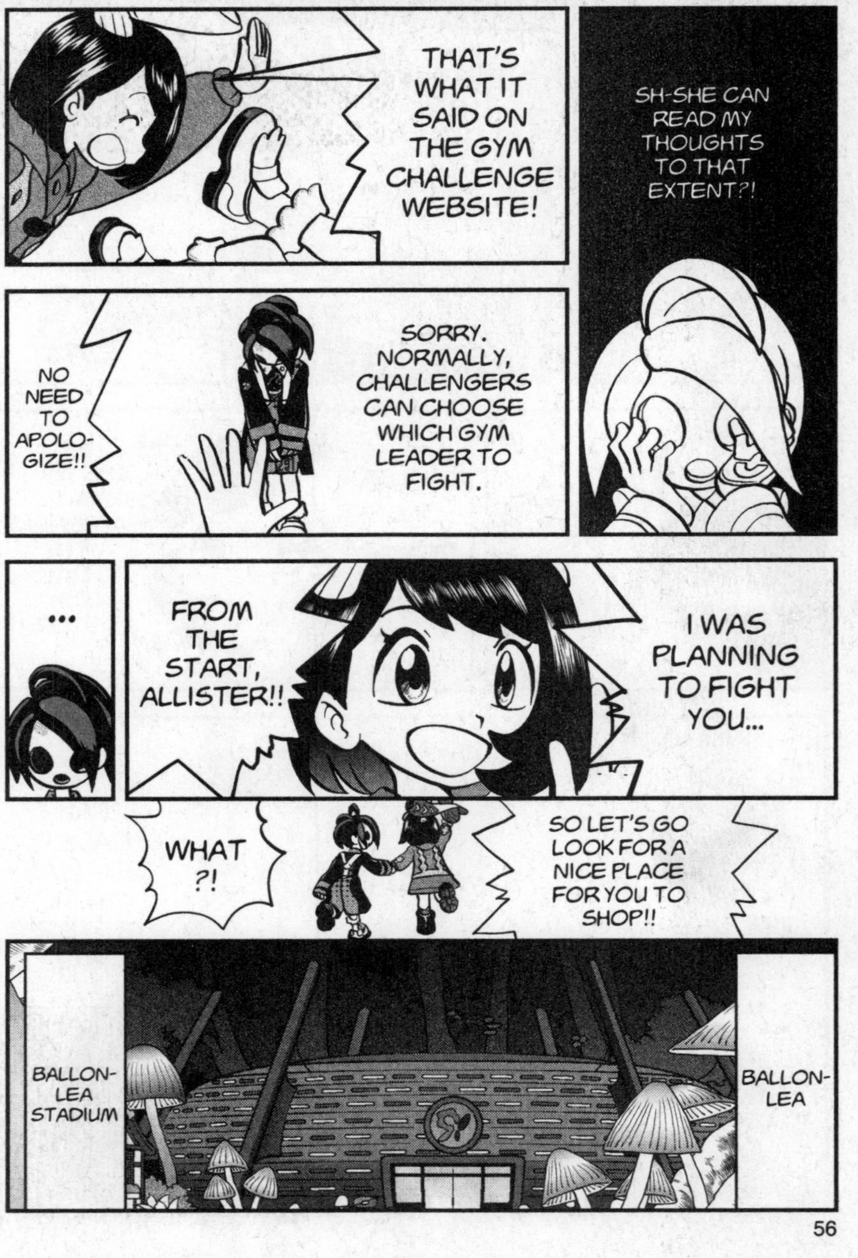
SH-SHE CAN READ MY THOUGHTS TO THAT EXTENT?!
THAT'S WHAT IT SAID ON THE GYM CHALLENGE WEBSITE!
SORRY. NORMALLY, CHALLENGERS CAN CHOOSE WHICH GYM LEADER TO FIGHT.
NO NEED TO APOLO-GIZE!!
I WAS PLANNING TO FIGHT YOU...
FROM THE START, ALLISTER!!
...
SO LET'S GO LOOK FOR A NICE PLACE FOR YOU TO SHOP!!
WHAT ?!
BALLON-LEA
BALLON-LEA STADIUM

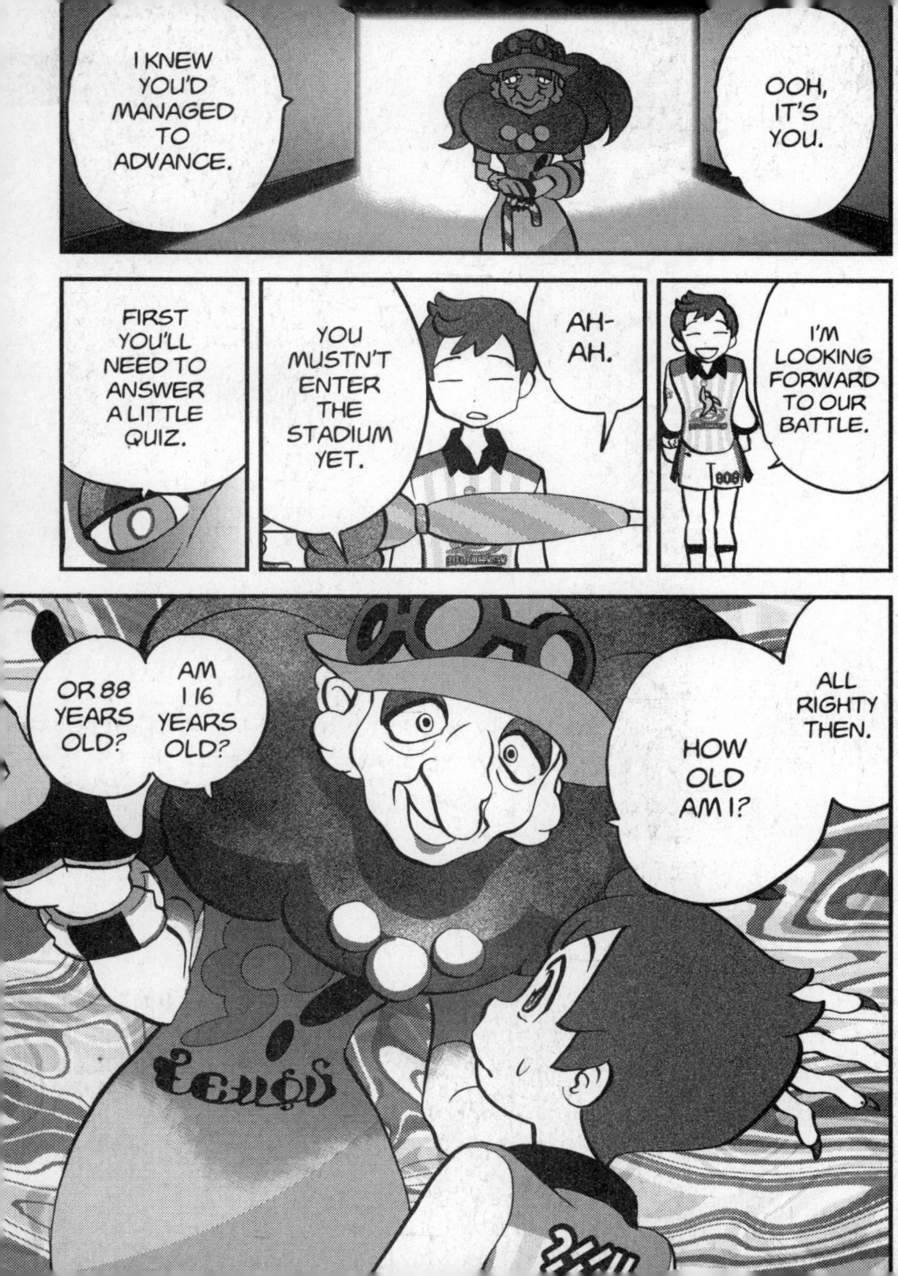
OOH, IT'S YOU.
I KNEW YOU'D MANAGED TO ADVANCE.
I'M LOOKING FORWARD TO OUR BATTLE.
AH-AH.
YOU MUSTN'T ENTER THE STADIUM YET.
FIRST YOU'LL NEED TO ANSWER A LITTLE QUIZ.
ALL RIGHTY THEN.
HOW OLD AM I?
AM I 16 YEARS OLD?
OR 88 YEARS OLD?

THE SECRETS OF DYNAMAX, PART 12

G-Max Move

G-Max Moves are moves that can only be used by a Gigantamaxed Pokémon.

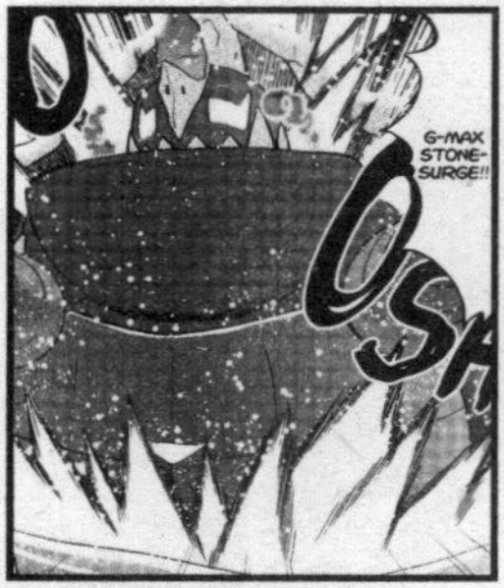
G-MAX STONE-SURGE!!

▲ **A special move that can only be used by Gigantamax Drednaw!**

Adventure 16 Rising!! Opal of Ballonlea

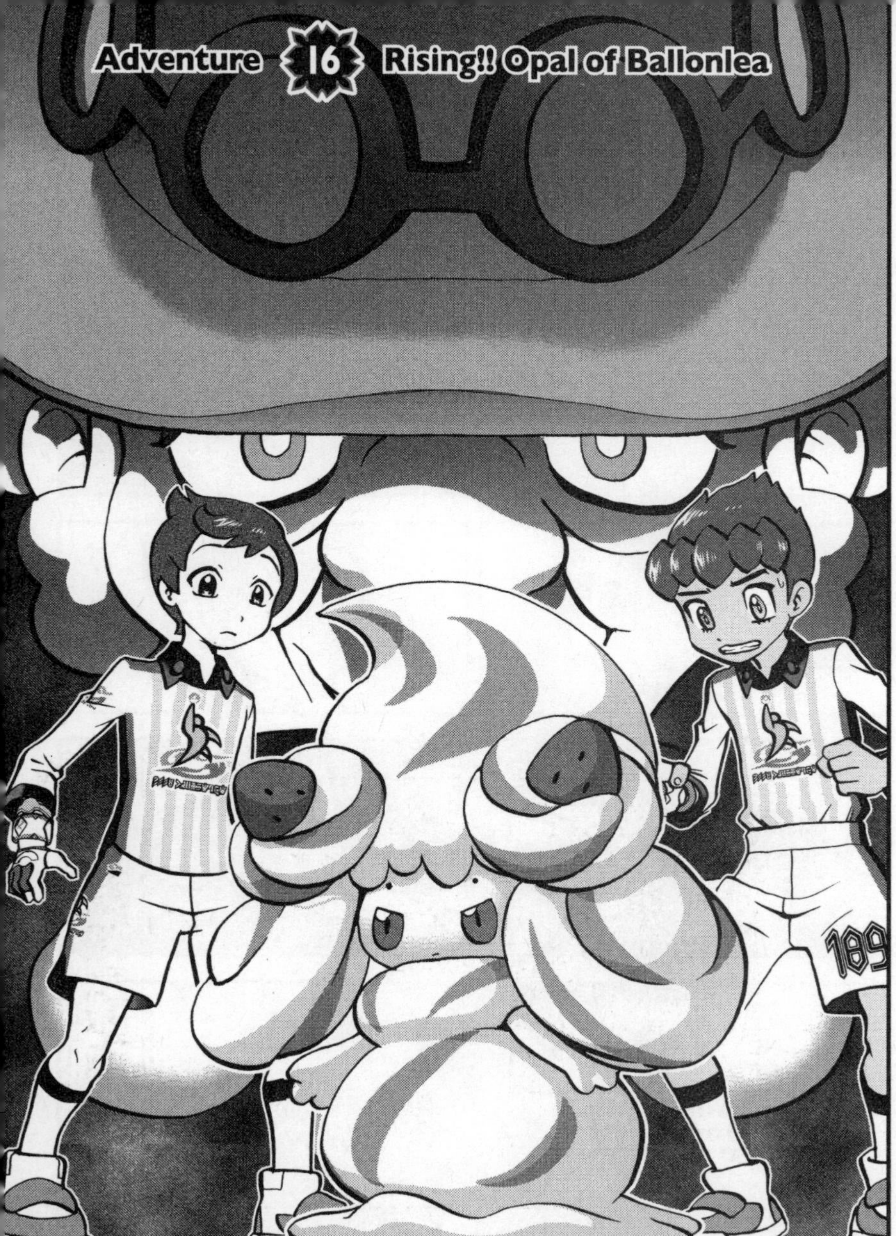
189

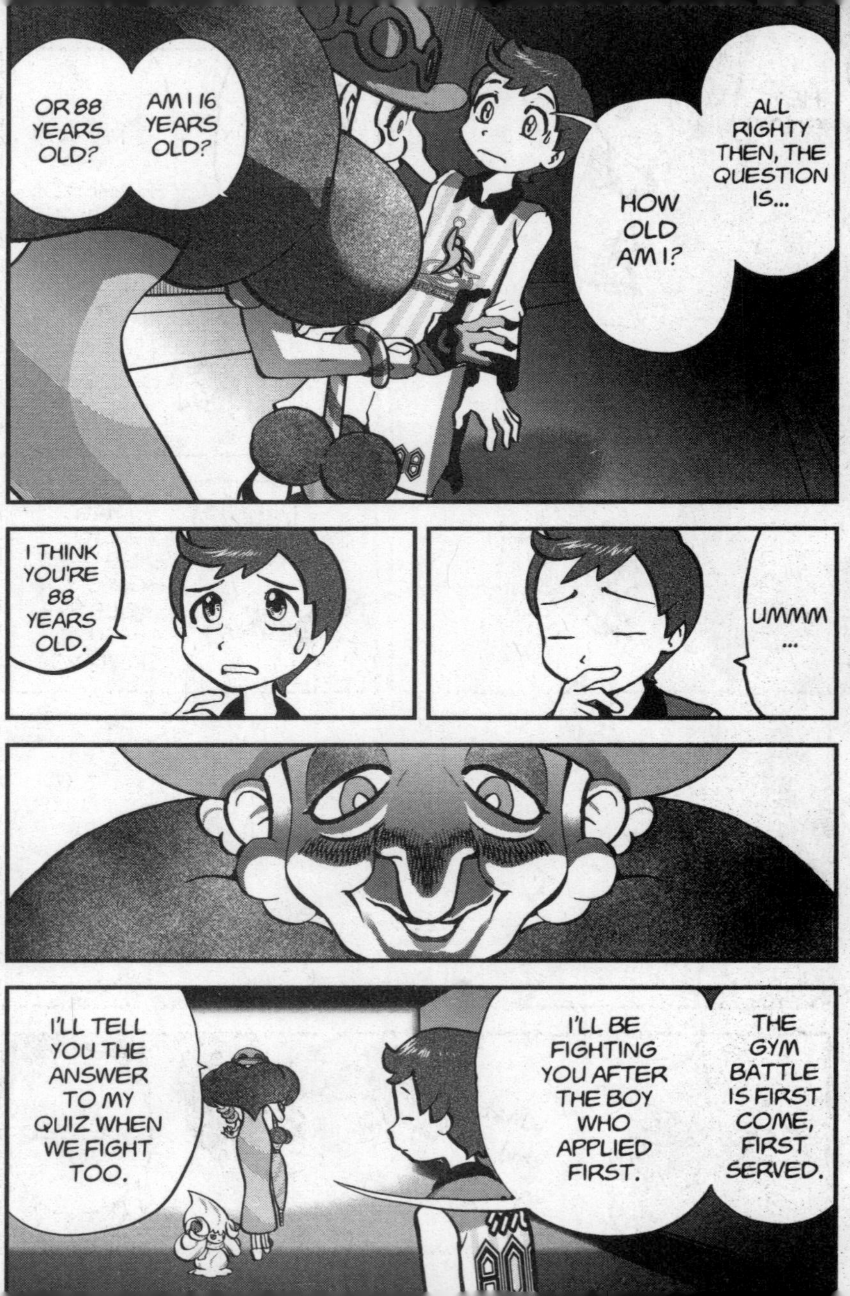
ALL RIGHTY THEN, THE QUESTION IS...
HOW OLD AM I?
AM I 16 YEARS OLD?
OR 88 YEARS OLD?
UMMM...
I THINK YOU'RE 88 YEARS OLD.
THE GYM BATTLE IS FIRST COME, FIRST SERVED.
I'LL BE FIGHTING YOU AFTER THE BOY WHO APPLIED FIRST.
I'LL TELL YOU THE ANSWER TO MY QUIZ WHEN WE FIGHT TOO.

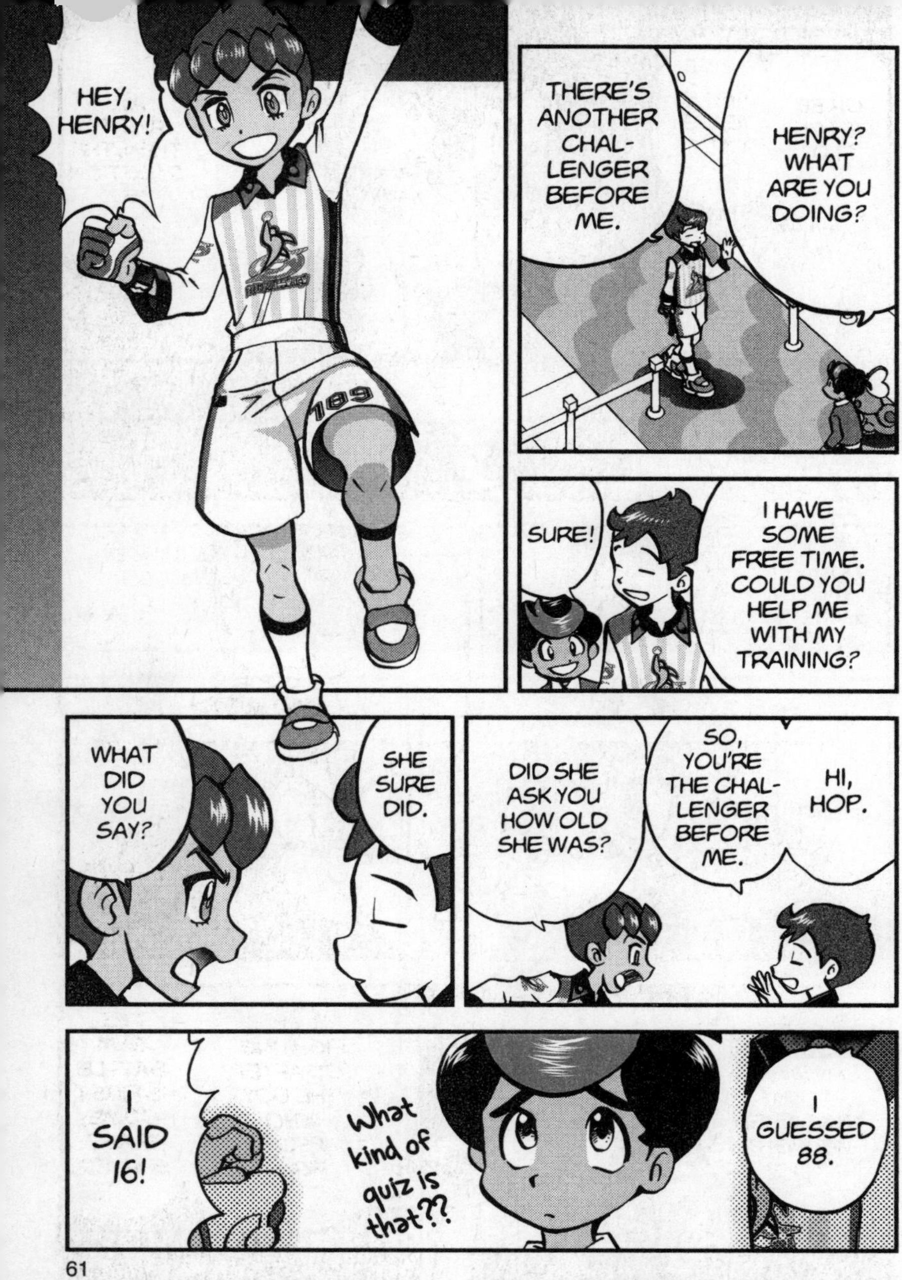
HENRY? WHAT ARE YOU DOING?
THERE'S ANOTHER CHAL-LENGER BEFORE ME.
I HAVE SOME FREE TIME. COULD YOU HELP ME WITH MY TRAINING?
SURE!
HEY, HENRY!
HI, HOP.
SO, YOU'RE THE CHAL-LENGER BEFORE ME.
DID SHE ASK YOU HOW OLD SHE WAS?
SHE SURE DID.
WHAT DID YOU SAY?
I GUESSED 88.
What kind of quiz is that??
I SAID 16!

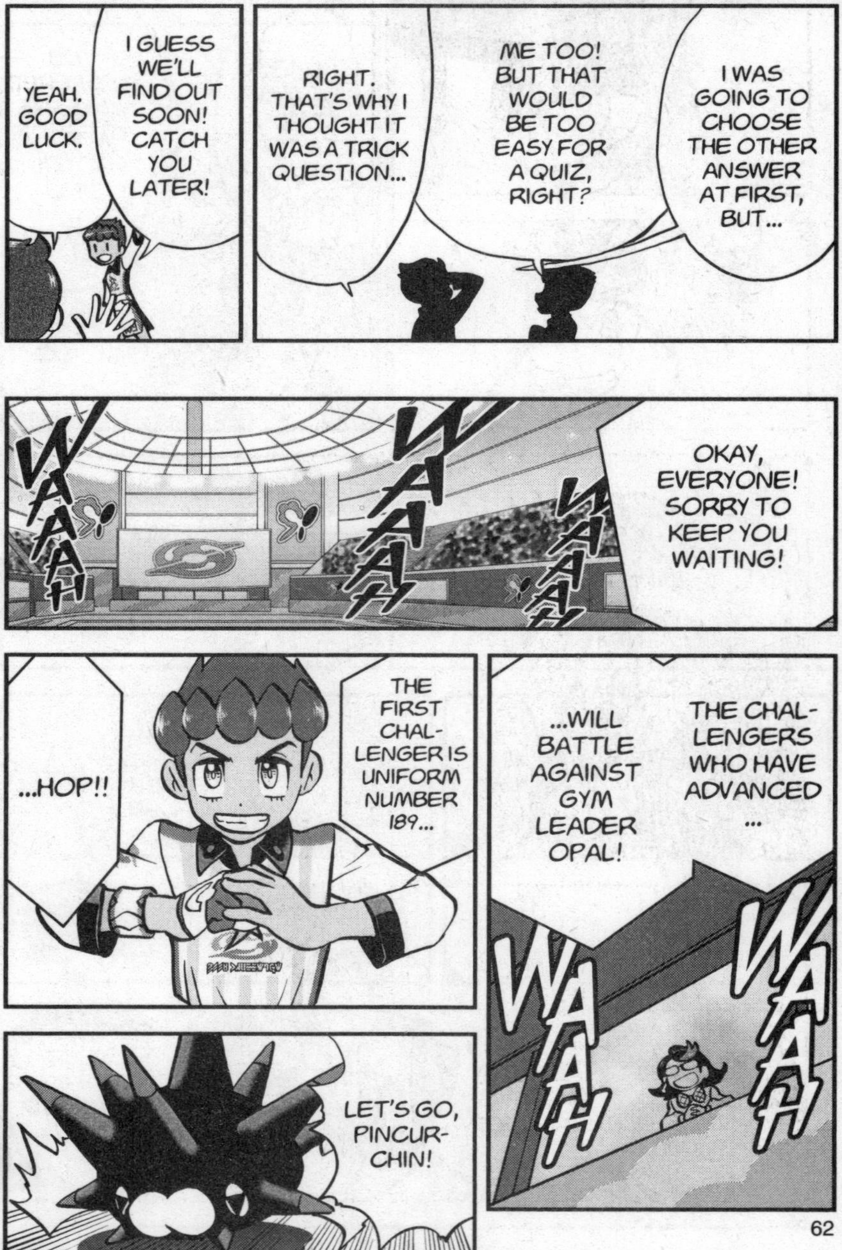

I WAS GOING TO CHOOSE THE OTHER ANSWER AT FIRST, BUT...
ME TOO! BUT THAT WOULD BE TOO EASY FOR A QUIZ, RIGHT?
RIGHT. THAT'S WHY I THOUGHT IT WAS A TRICK QUESTION...
I GUESS WE'LL FIND OUT SOON! CATCH YOU LATER!
YEAH. GOOD LUCK.
OKAY, EVERYONE! SORRY TO KEEP YOU WAITING!
WAAAH
WAAAH
WAAAH
THE CHAL-LENGERS WHO HAVE ADVANCED ...
...WILL BATTLE AGAINST GYM LEADER OPAL!
WAAAH
WAAAH
THE FIRST CHAL-LENGER IS UNIFORM NUMBER 189...
...HOP!!
LET'S GO, PINCUR-CHIN!

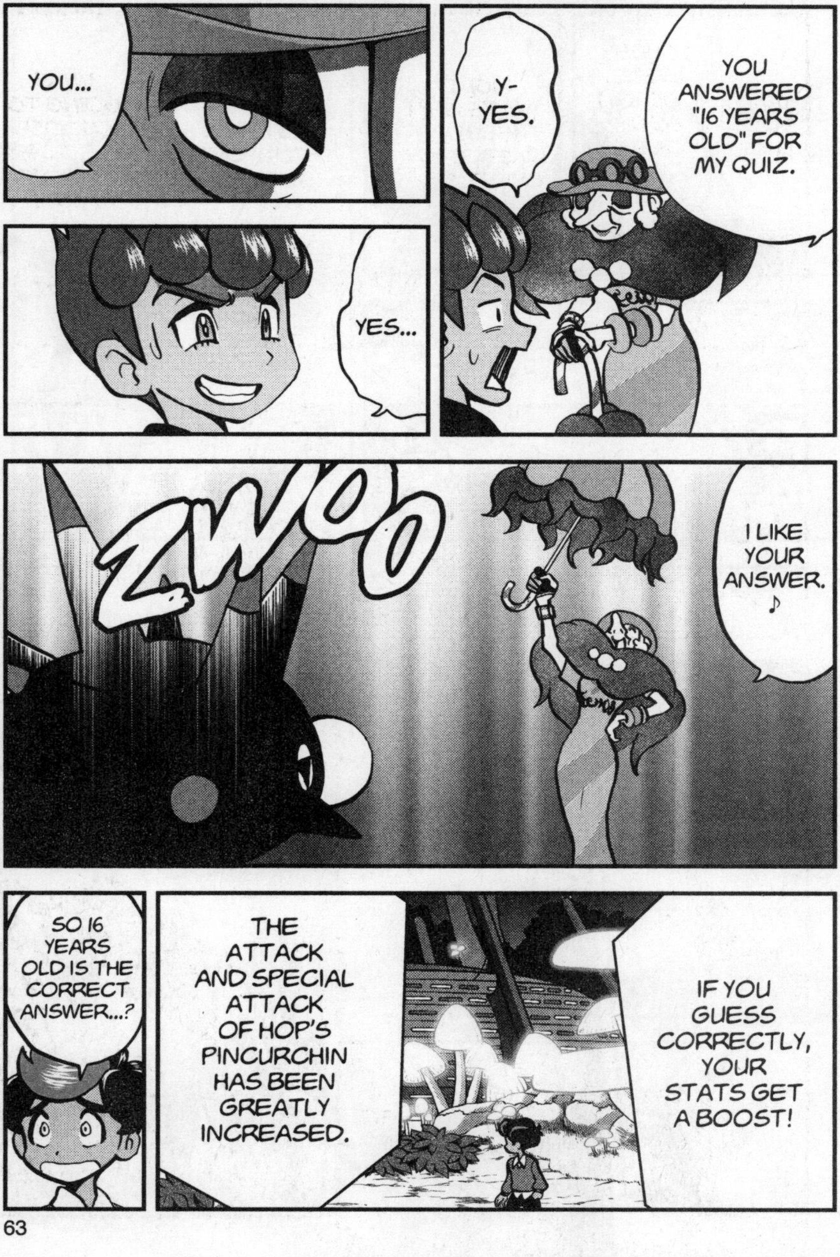
YOU ANSWERED "16 YEARS OLD" FOR MY QUIZ.
Y- YES.
YOU...
YES...
I LIKE YOUR ANSWER. ♪
ZWOO
IF YOU GUESS CORRECTLY, YOUR STATS GET A BOOST!
THE ATTACK AND SPECIAL ATTACK OF HOP'S PINCURCHIN HAS BEEN GREATLY INCREASED.
SO 16 YEARS OLD IS THE CORRECT ANSWER...?

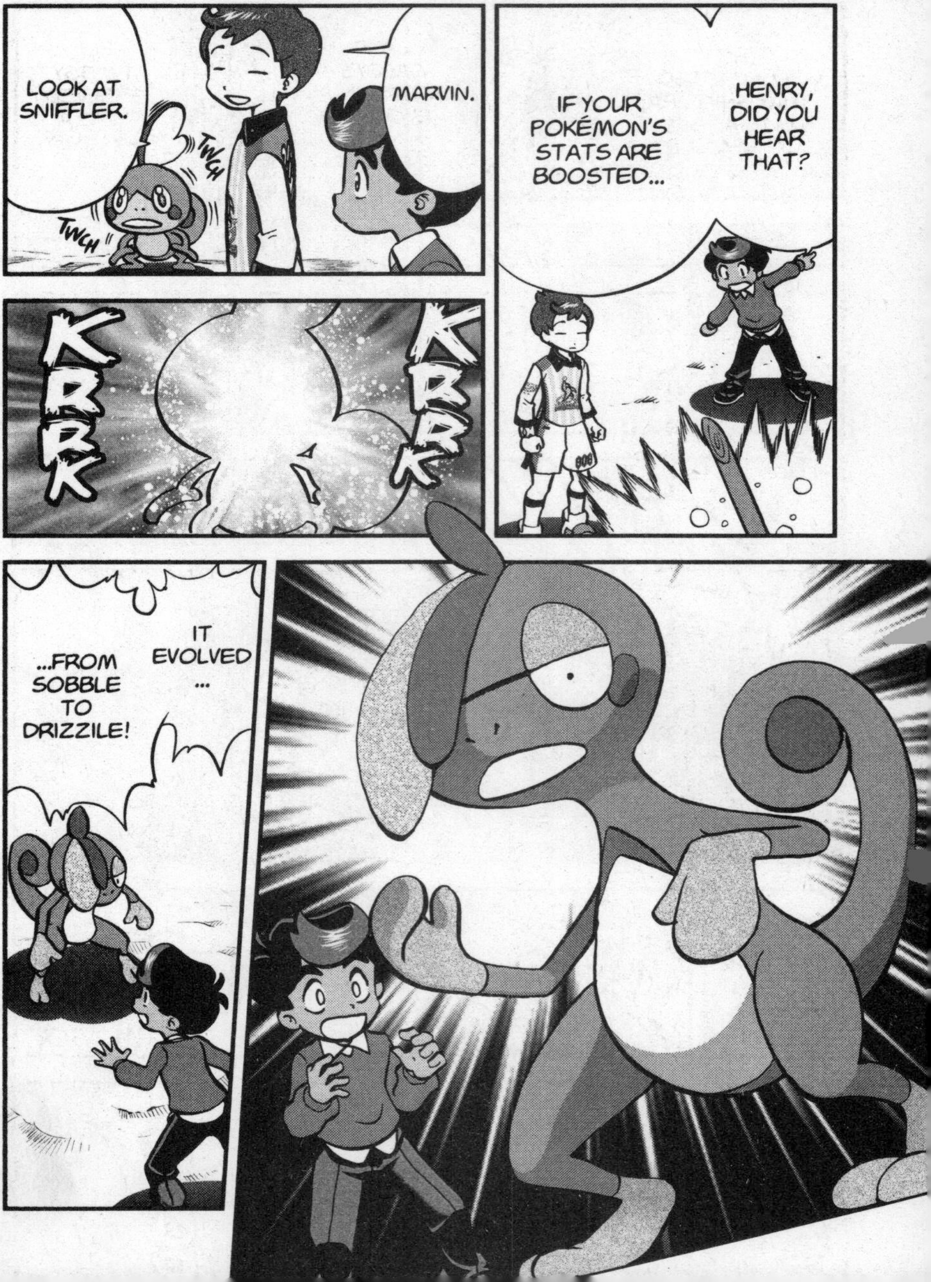
HENRY, DID YOU HEAR THAT?
IF YOUR POKÉMON'S STATS ARE BOOSTED...
MARVIN.
TWCH
LOOK AT SNIFFLER.
TWCH
KRBRK
KRBRK
IT EVOLVED...
...FROM SOBBLE TO DRIZZILE!

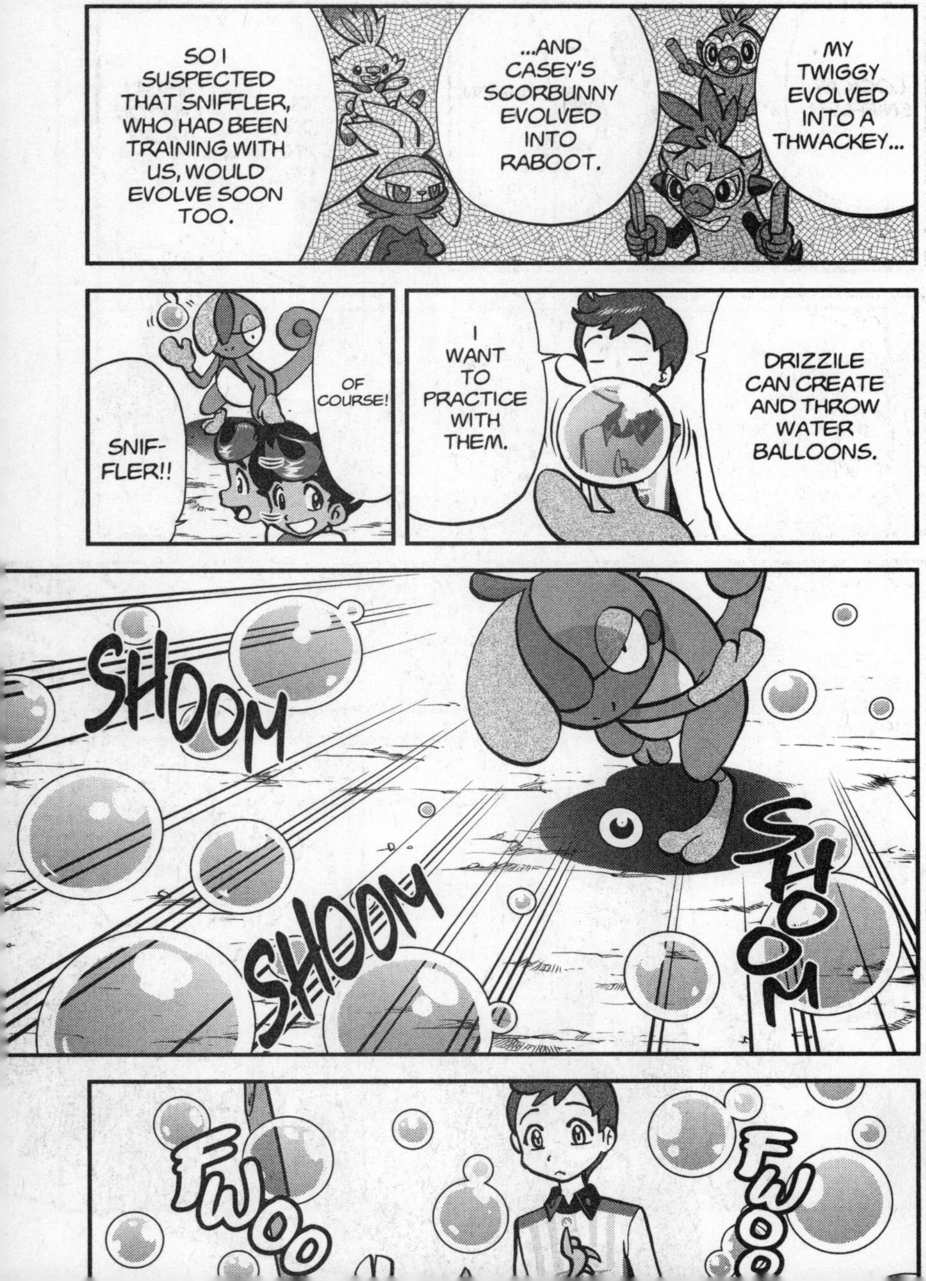
MY TWIGGY EVOLVED INTO A THWACKEY...
...AND CASEY'S SCORBUNNY EVOLVED INTO RABOOT.
SO I SUSPECTED THAT SNIFFLER, WHO HAD BEEN TRAINING WITH US, WOULD EVOLVE SOON TOO.
DRIZZILE CAN CREATE AND THROW WATER BALLOONS.
I WANT TO PRACTICE WITH THEM.
OF COURSE!
SNIF-FLER!!
SHOOM
SHOOM
SHOOM
FWOO
FWOO

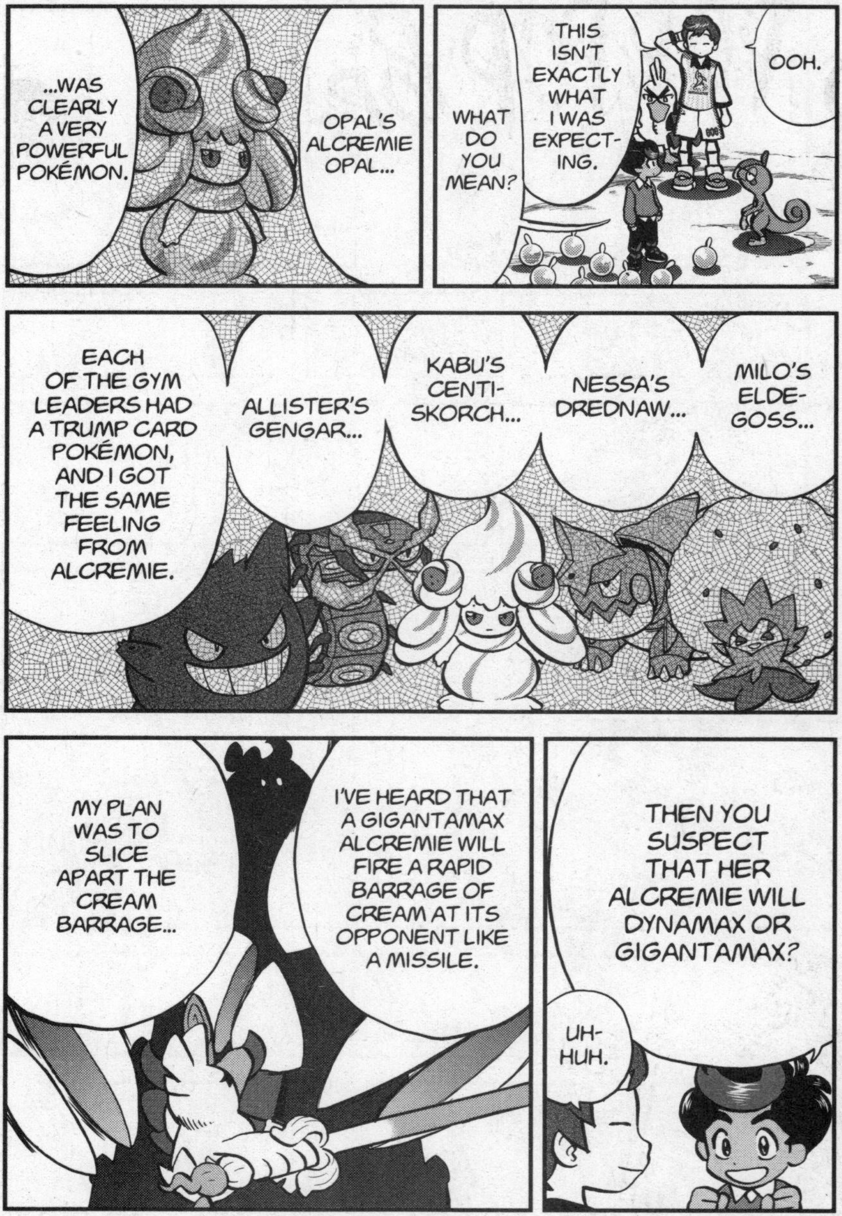
OOH.
THIS ISN'T EXACTLY WHAT I WAS EXPECTING.
WHAT DO YOU MEAN?
OPAL'S ALCREMIE OPAL...
...WAS CLEARLY A VERY POWERFUL POKÉMON.
MILO'S ELDEGOSS...
NESSA'S DREDNAW...
KABU'S CENTISKORCH...
ALLISTER'S GENGAR...
EACH OF THE GYM LEADERS HAD A TRUMP CARD POKÉMON, AND I GOT THE SAME FEELING FROM ALCREMIE.
THEN YOU SUSPECT THAT HER ALCREMIE WILL DYNAMAX OR GIGANTAMAX?
UH-HUH.
I'VE HEARD THAT A GIGANTAMAX ALCREMIE WILL FIRE A RAPID BARRAGE OF CREAM AT ITS OPPONENT LIKE A MISSILE.
MY PLAN WAS TO SLICE APART THE CREAM BARRAGE...

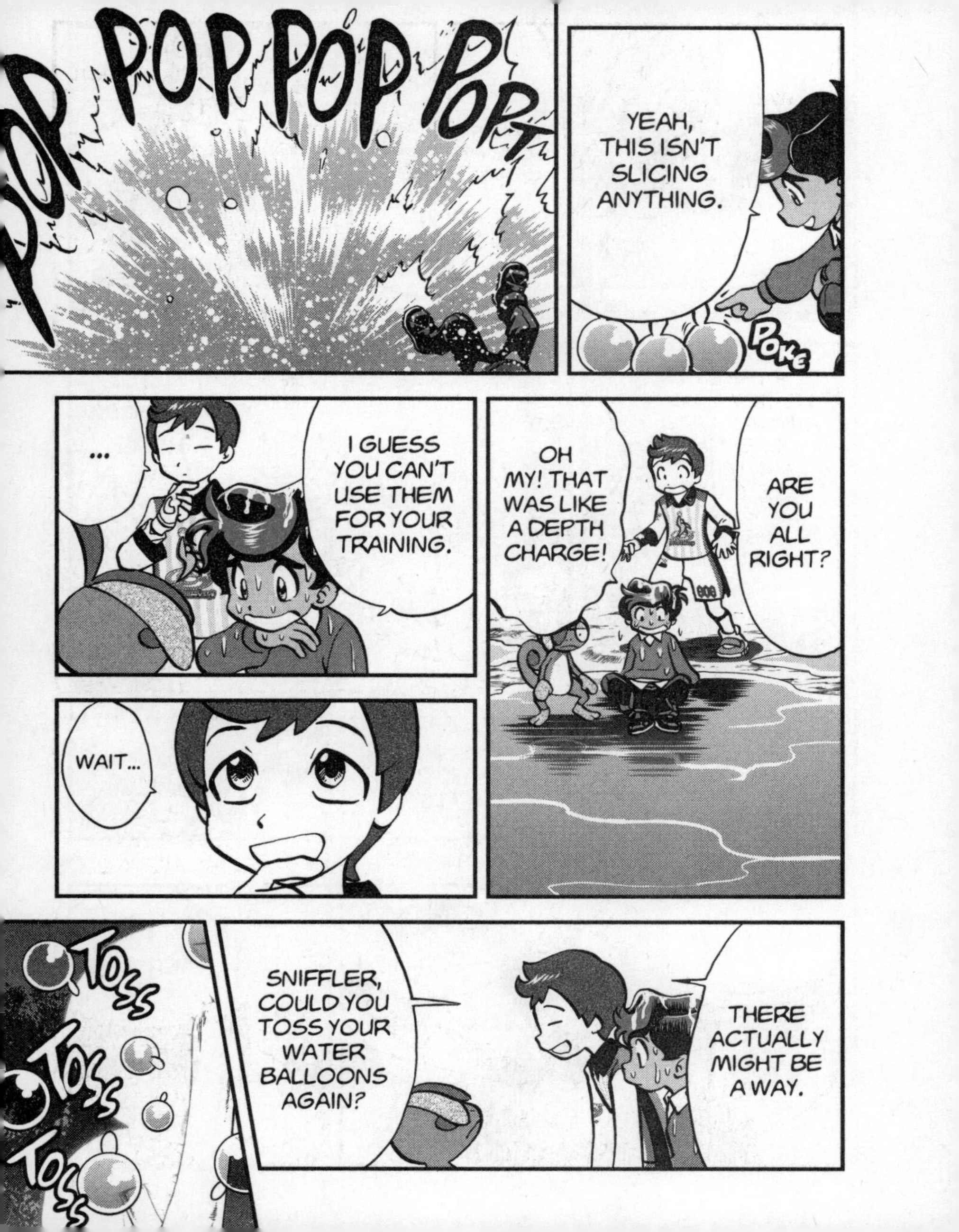
YEAH, THIS ISN'T SLICING ANYTHING.
POKE
POP POP POP POP POP
ARE YOU ALL RIGHT?
OH MY! THAT WAS LIKE A DEPTH CHARGE!
I GUESS YOU CAN'T USE THEM FOR YOUR TRAINING.
...
WAIT...
THERE ACTUALLY MIGHT BE A WAY.
SNIFFLER, COULD YOU TOSS YOUR WATER BALLOONS AGAIN?
TOSS
TOSS
TOSS

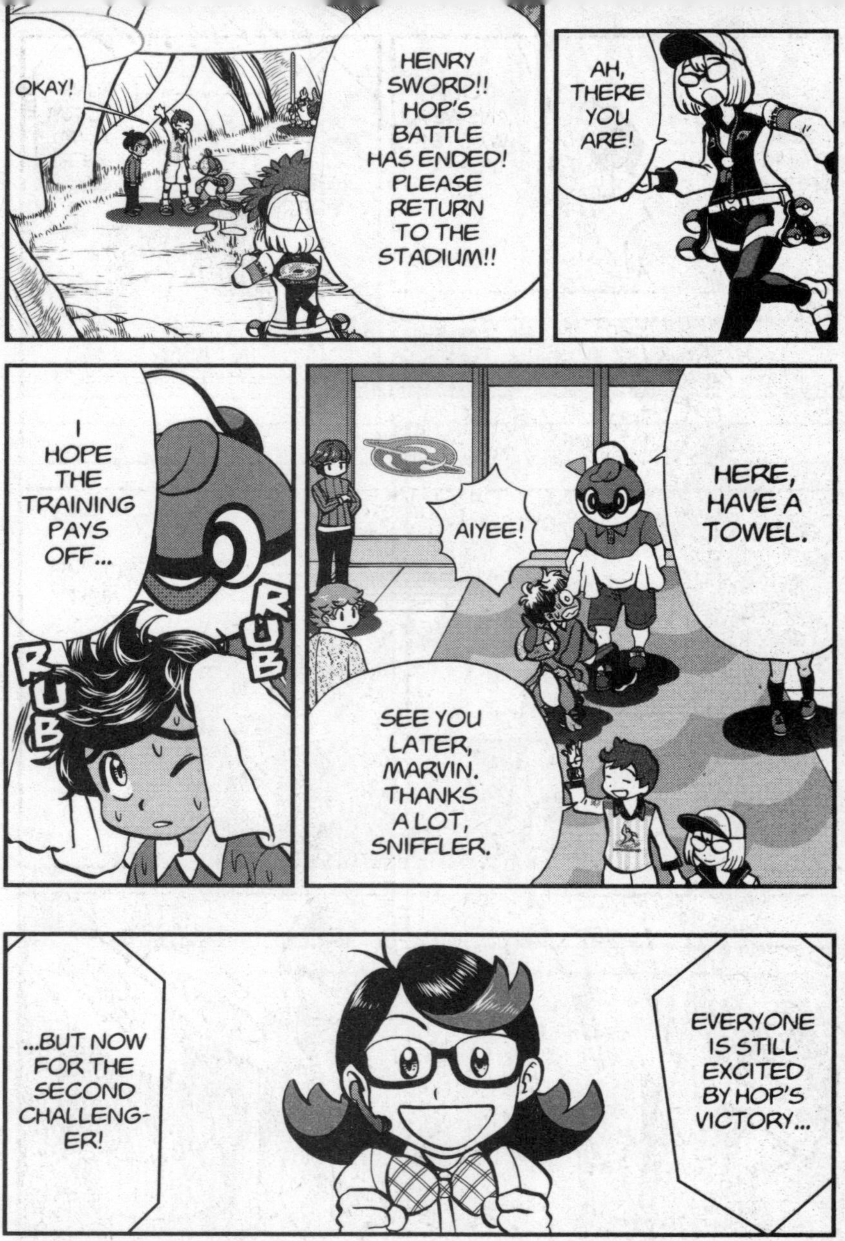
AH, THERE YOU ARE!
HENRY SWORD!! HOP'S BATTLE HAS ENDED! PLEASE RETURN TO THE STADIUM!!
OKAY!
HERE, HAVE A TOWEL.
AIYEE!
SEE YOU LATER, MARVIN. THANKS A LOT, SNIFFLER.
I HOPE THE TRAINING PAYS OFF...
RUB
RUB
EVERYONE IS STILL EXCITED BY HOP'S VICTORY...
...BUT NOW FOR THE SECOND CHALLENGER!

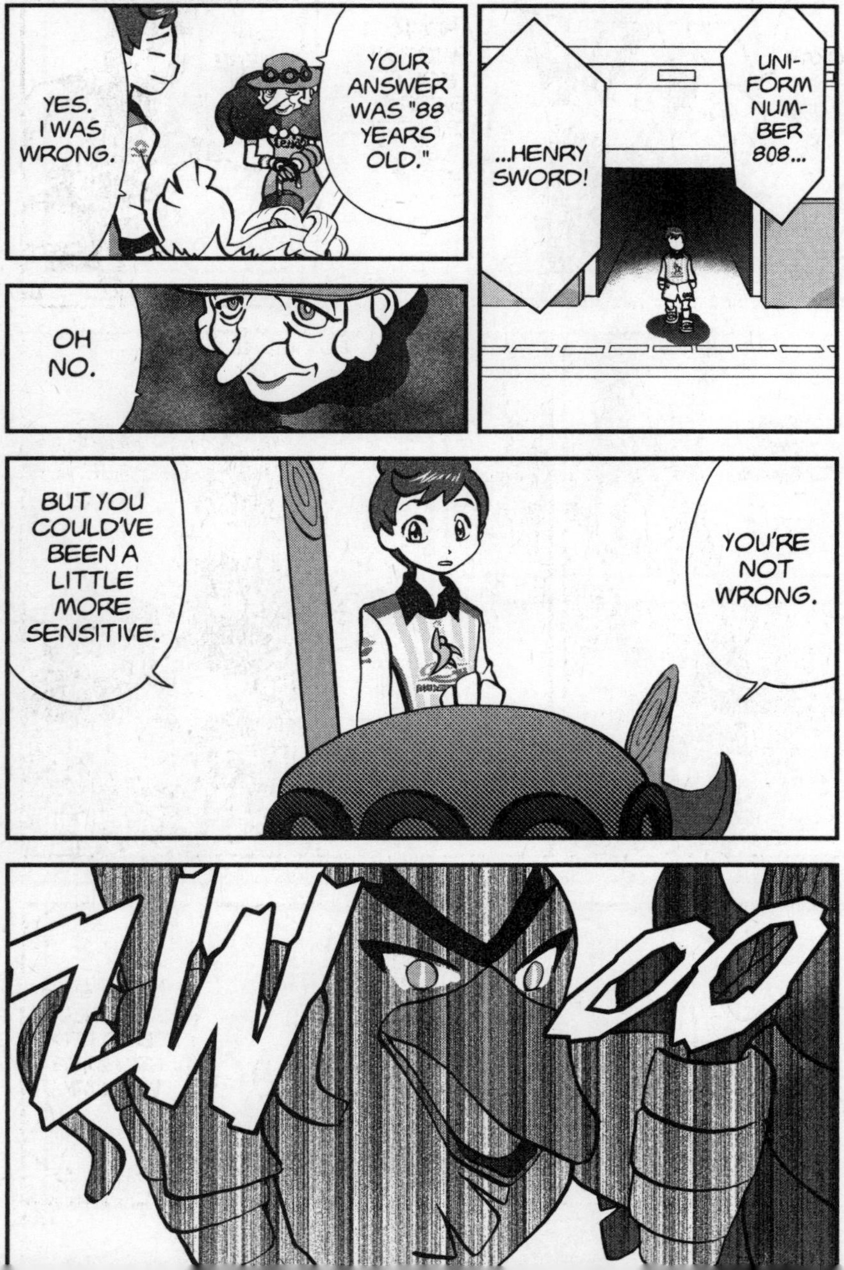

UNI-FORM NUM-BER 808...
...HENRY SWORD!
YOUR ANSWER WAS "88 YEARS OLD."
YES. I WAS WRONG.
OH NO.
YOU'RE NOT WRONG.
BUT YOU COULD'VE BEEN A LITTLE MORE SENSITIVE.
ZWOO

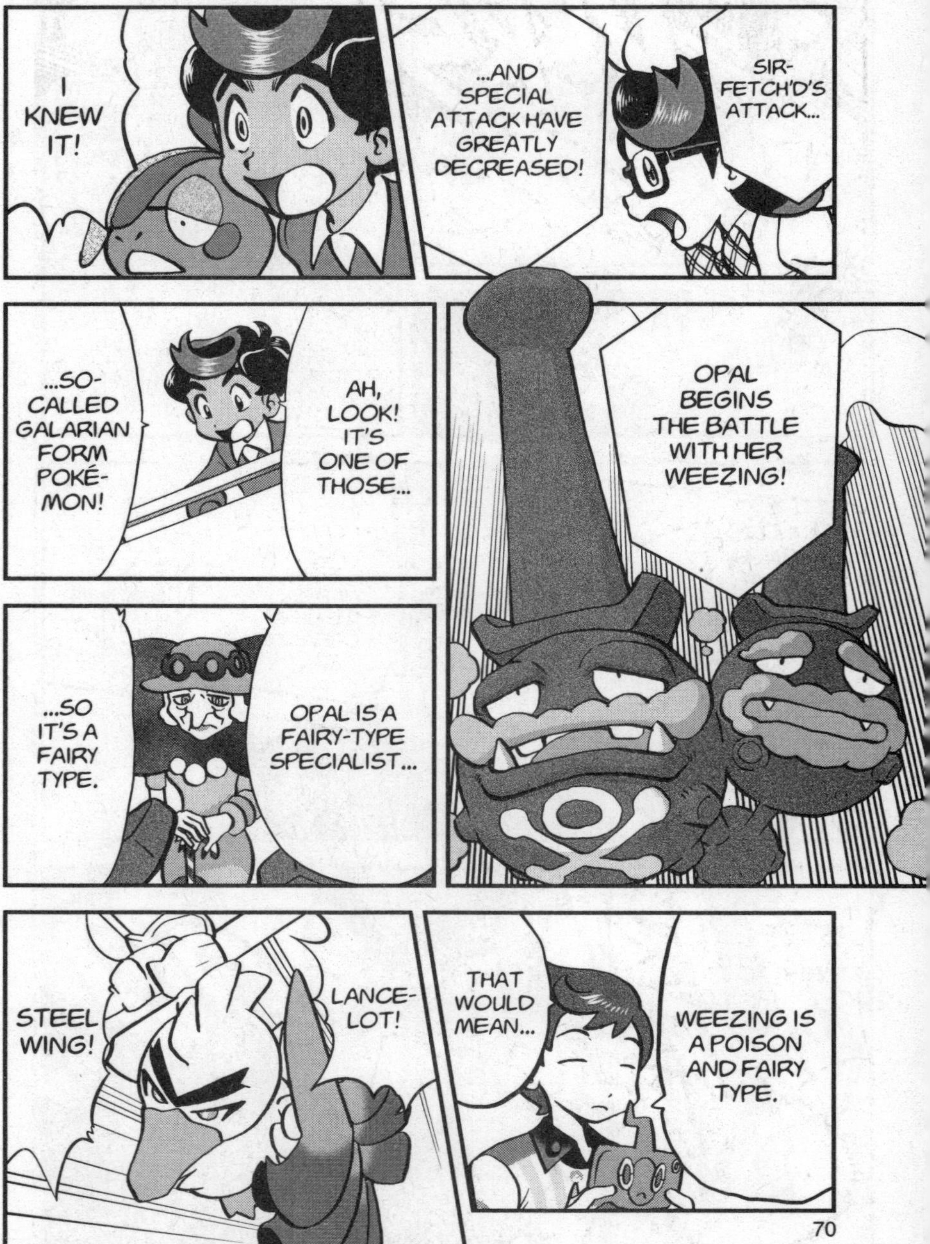
SIR-FETCH'D'S ATTACK...
...AND SPECIAL ATTACK HAVE GREATLY DECREASED!
I KNEW IT!
OPAL BEGINS THE BATTLE WITH HER WEEZING!
AH, LOOK! IT'S ONE OF THOSE...
...SO-CALLED GALARIAN FORM POKÉ-MON!
OPAL IS A FAIRY-TYPE SPECIALIST...
...SO IT'S A FAIRY TYPE.
WEEZING IS A POISON AND FAIRY TYPE.
THAT WOULD MEAN...
LANCE-LOT!
STEEL WING!

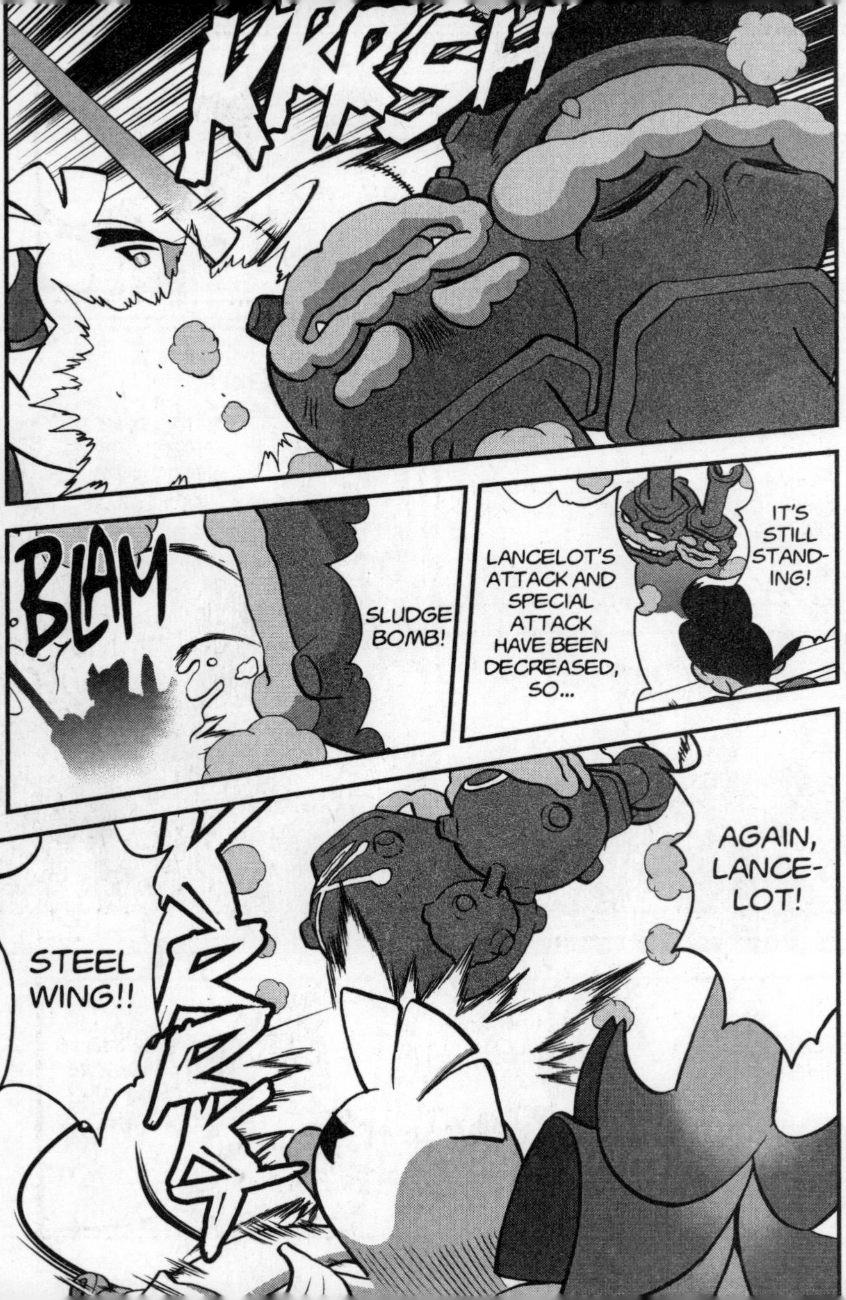
KRRSH
IT'S STILL STAND-ING!
LANCELOT'S ATTACK AND SPECIAL ATTACK HAVE BEEN DECREASED, SO...
SLUDGE BOMB!
BLAM
AGAIN, LANCE-LOT!
STEEL WING!!

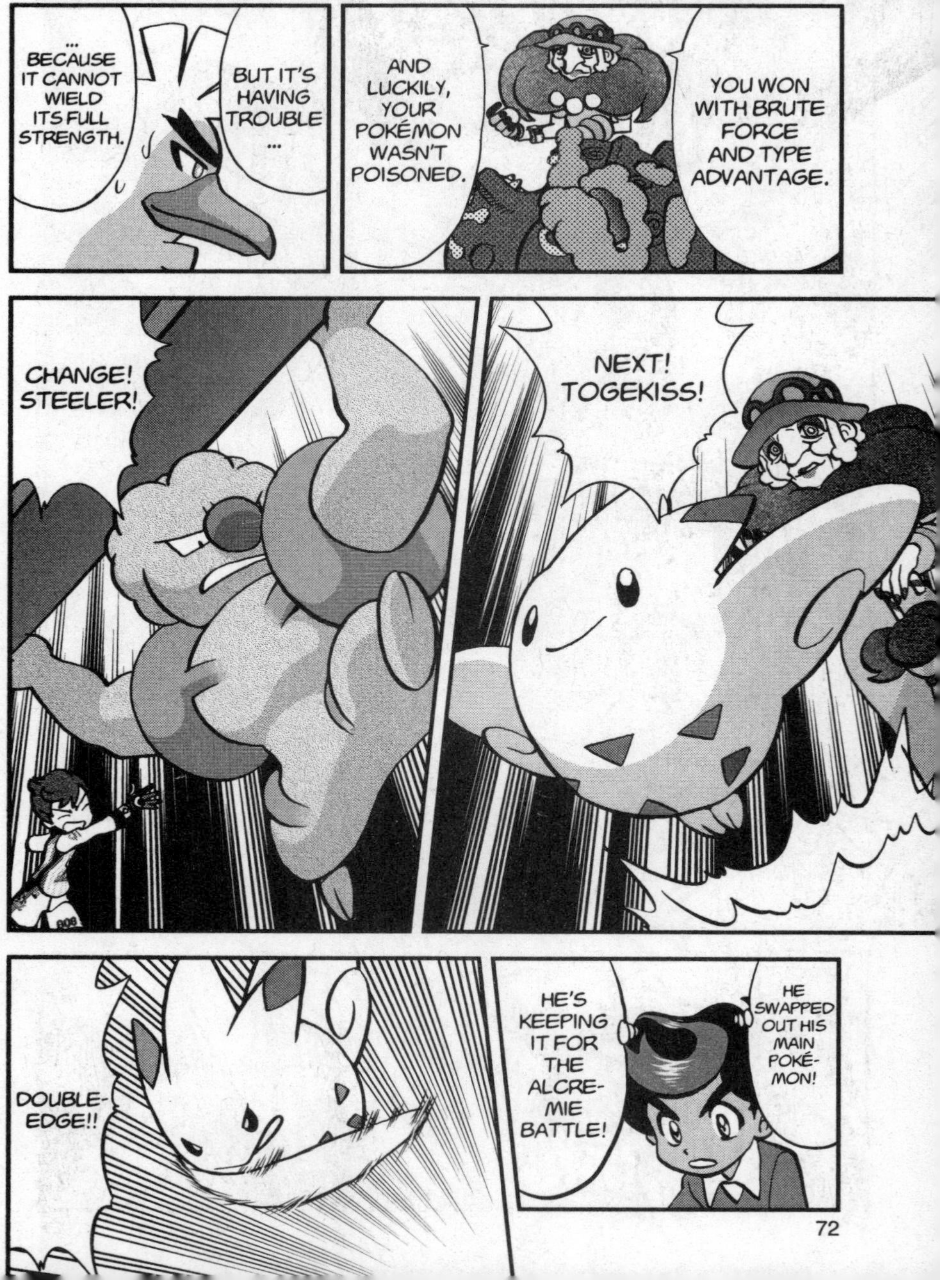
YOU WON WITH BRUTE FORCE AND TYPE ADVANTAGE.
AND LUCKILY, YOUR POKÉMON WASN'T POISONED.
BUT IT'S HAVING TROUBLE ...
... BECAUSE IT CANNOT WIELD ITS FULL STRENGTH.
NEXT! TOGEKISS!
CHANGE! STEELER!
HE SWAPPED OUT HIS MAIN POKÉ-MON!
HE'S KEEPING IT FOR THE ALCRE-MIE BATTLE!
DOUBLE-EDGE!!

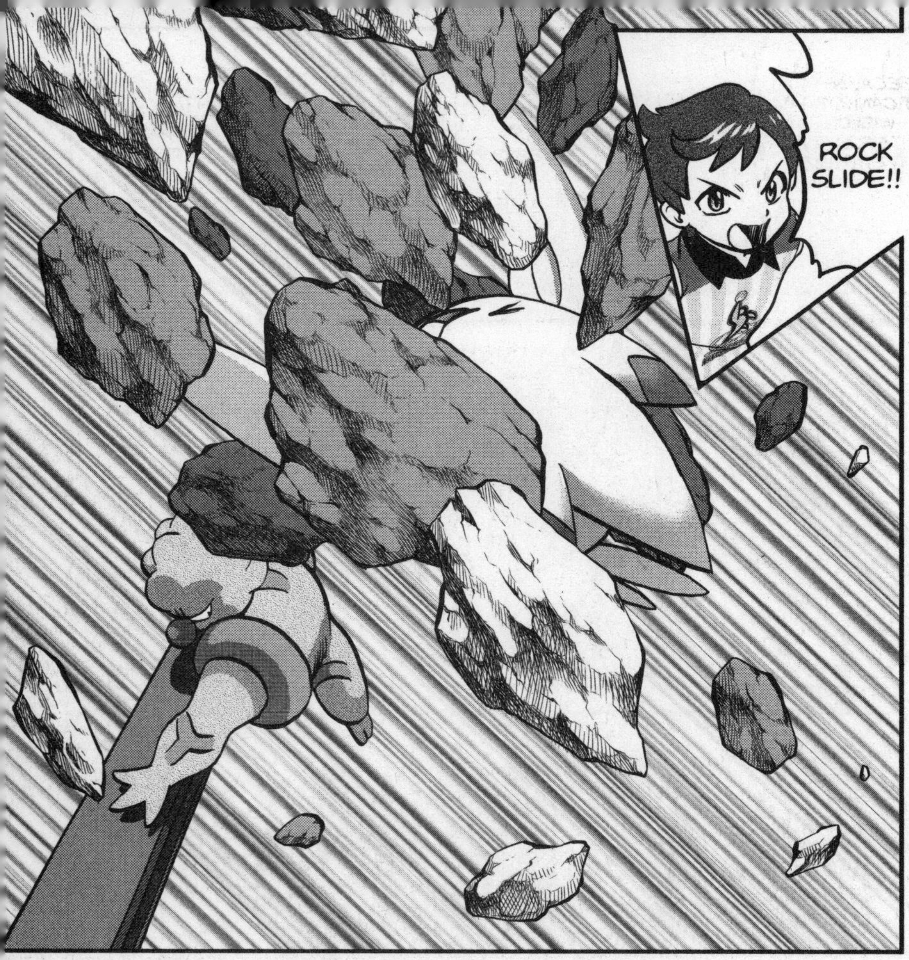
ROCK SLIDE!!
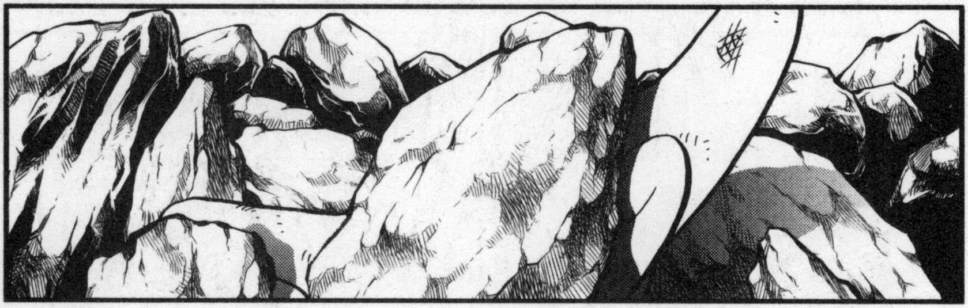

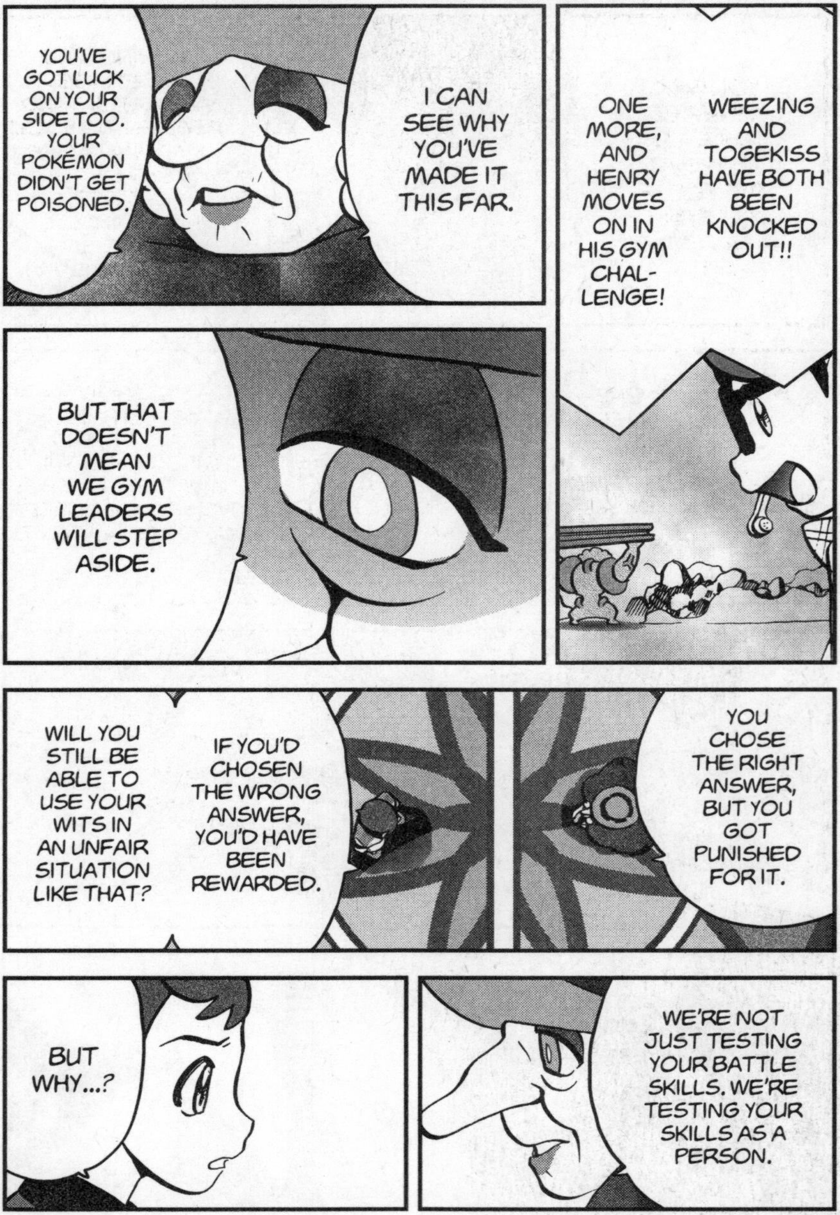
WEEZING AND TOGEKISS HAVE BOTH BEEN KNOCKED OUT!!
ONE MORE, AND HENRY MOVES ON IN HIS GYM CHAL-LENGE!
I CAN SEE WHY YOU'VE MADE IT THIS FAR.
YOU'VE GOT LUCK ON YOUR SIDE TOO. YOUR POKÉMON DIDN'T GET POISONED.
BUT THAT DOESN'T MEAN WE GYM LEADERS WILL STEP ASIDE.
YOU CHOSE THE RIGHT ANSWER, BUT YOU GOT PUNISHED FOR IT.
IF YOU'D CHOSEN THE WRONG ANSWER, YOU'D HAVE BEEN REWARDED.
WILL YOU STILL BE ABLE TO USE YOUR WITS IN AN UNFAIR SITUATION LIKE THAT?
WE'RE NOT JUST TESTING YOUR BATTLE SKILLS. WE'RE TESTING YOUR SKILLS AS A PERSON.
BUT WHY...?

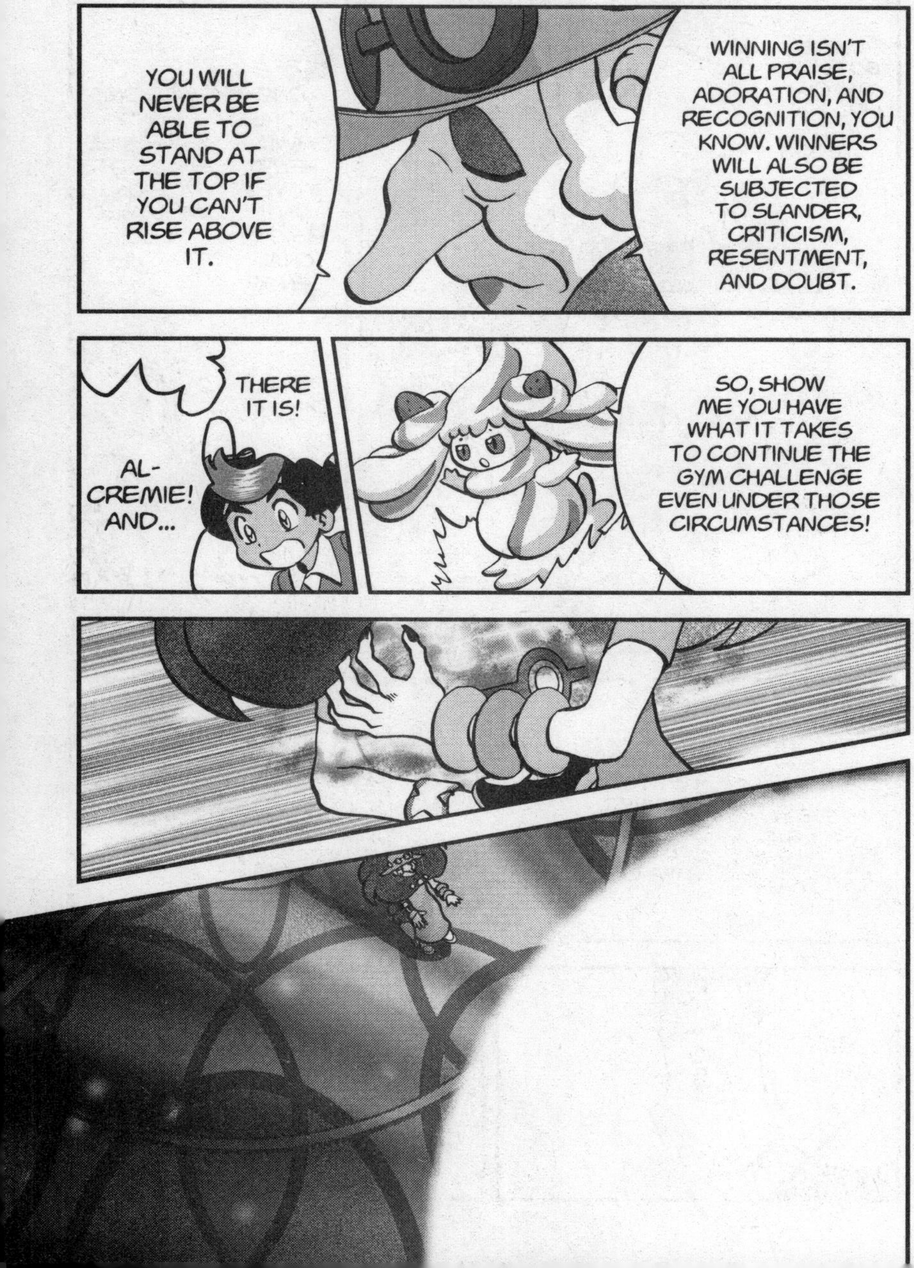
WINNING ISN'T ALL PRAISE, ADORATION, AND RECOGNITION, YOU KNOW. WINNERS WILL ALSO BE SUBJECTED TO SLANDER, CRITICISM, RESENTMENT, AND DOUBT.
YOU WILL NEVER BE ABLE TO STAND AT THE TOP IF YOU CAN'T RISE ABOVE IT.
SO, SHOW ME YOU HAVE WHAT IT TAKES TO CONTINUE THE GYM CHALLENGE EVEN UNDER THOSE CIRCUMSTANCES!
THERE IT IS!
AL-CREMIE! AND...

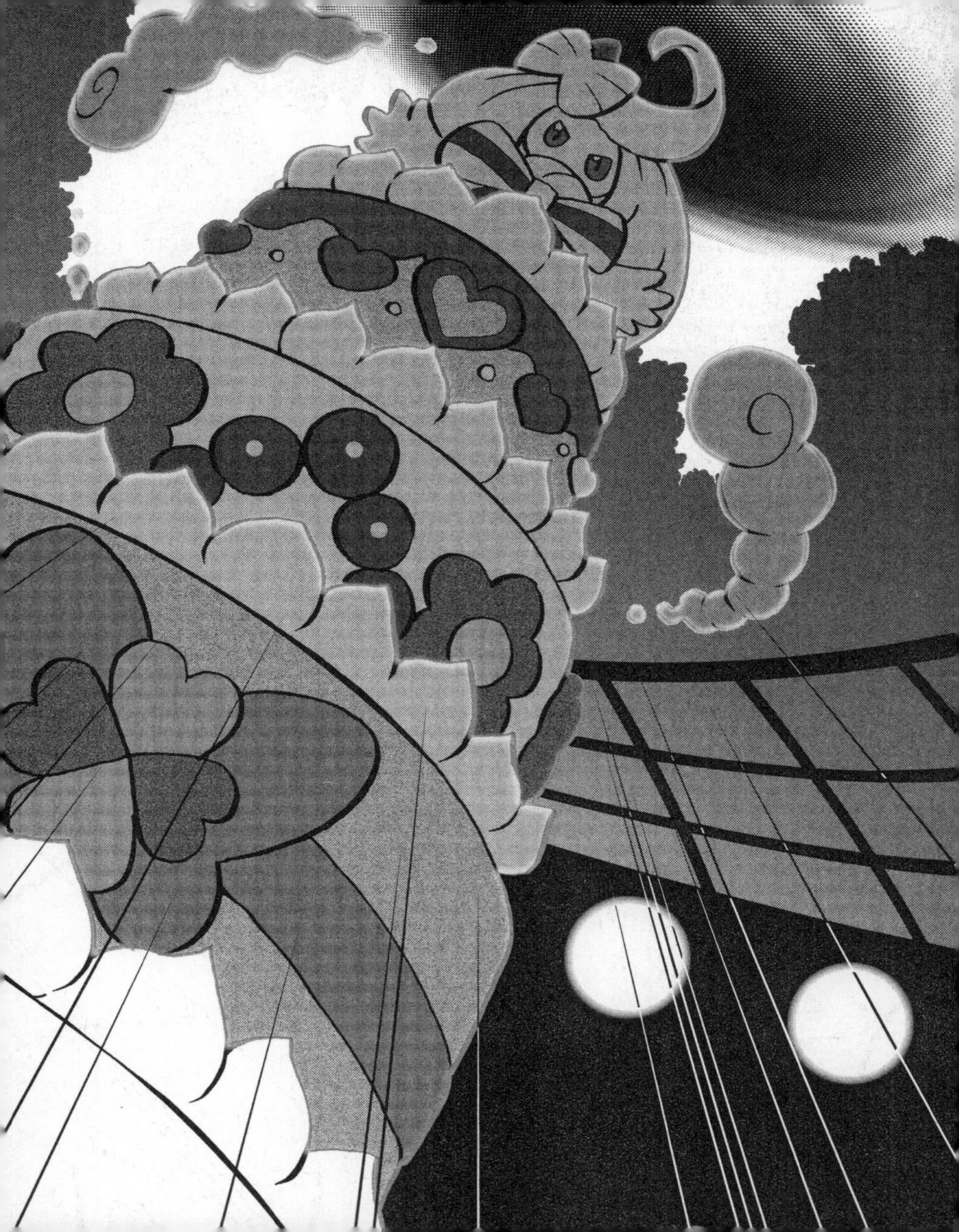

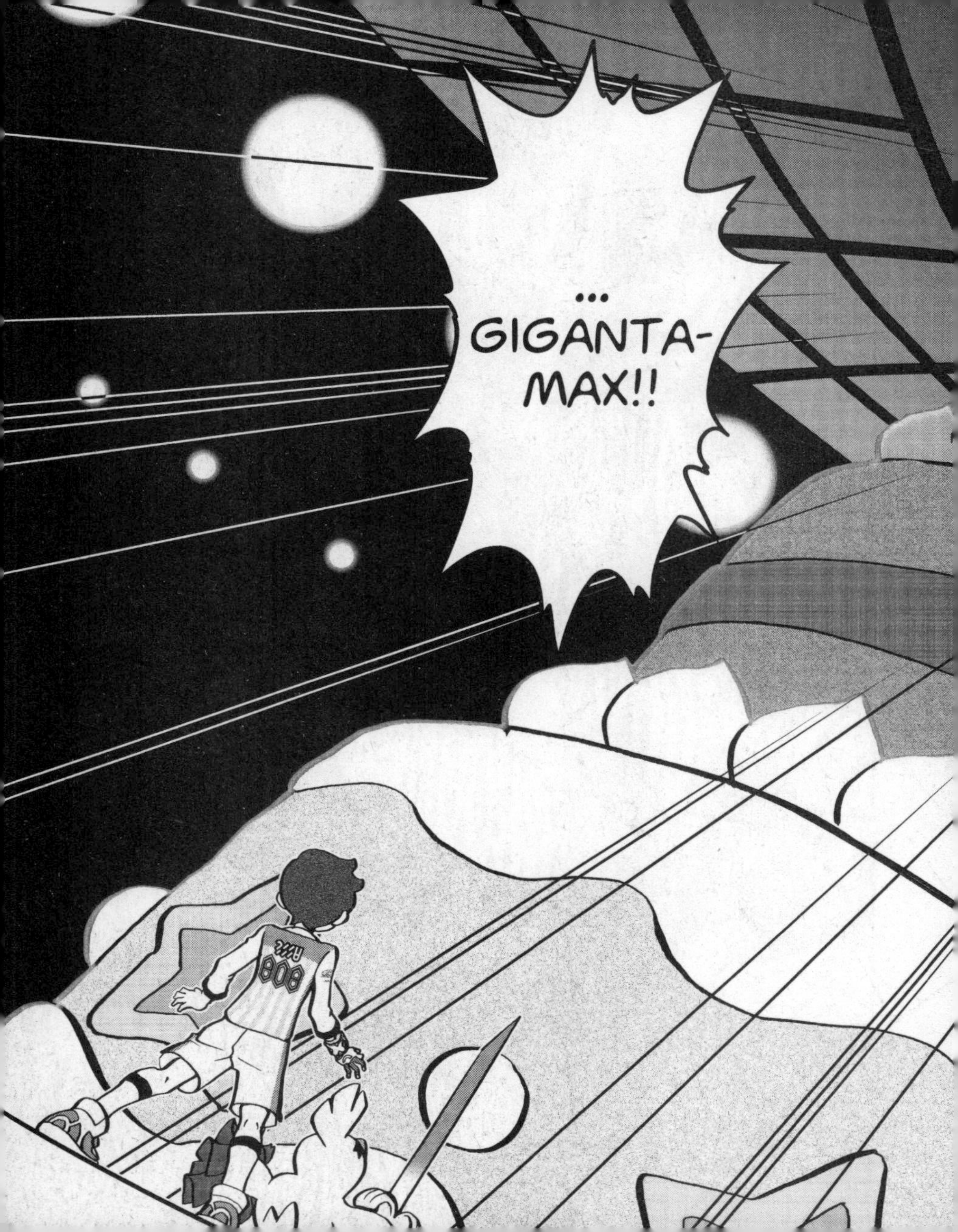
... GIGANTA-MAX!!

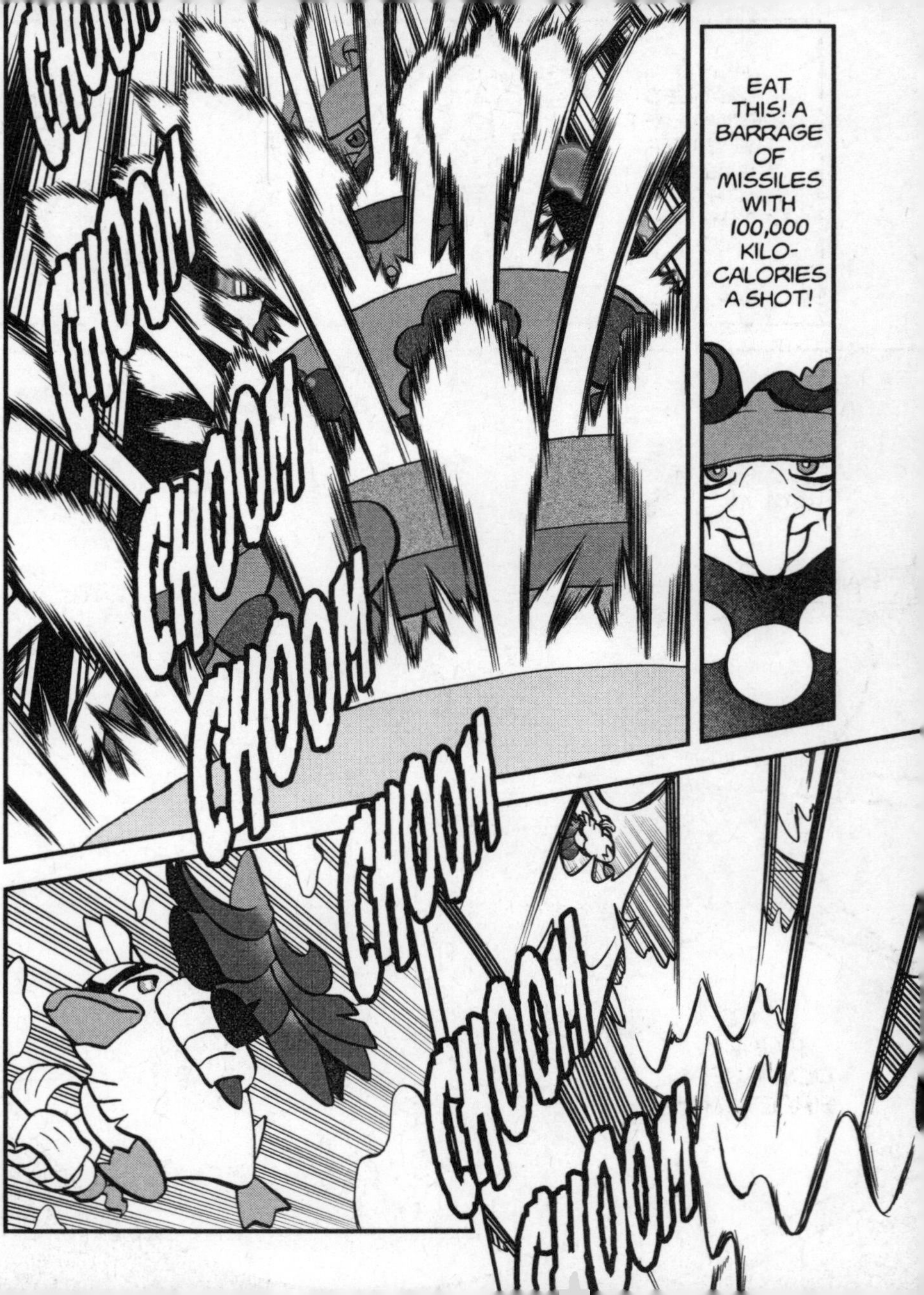
EAT THIS! A BARRAGE OF MISSILES WITH 100,000 KILO-CALORIES A SHOT!
CHOOM
CHOOM
CHOOM
CHOOM
CHOOM
CHOOM
CHOOM
CHOOM

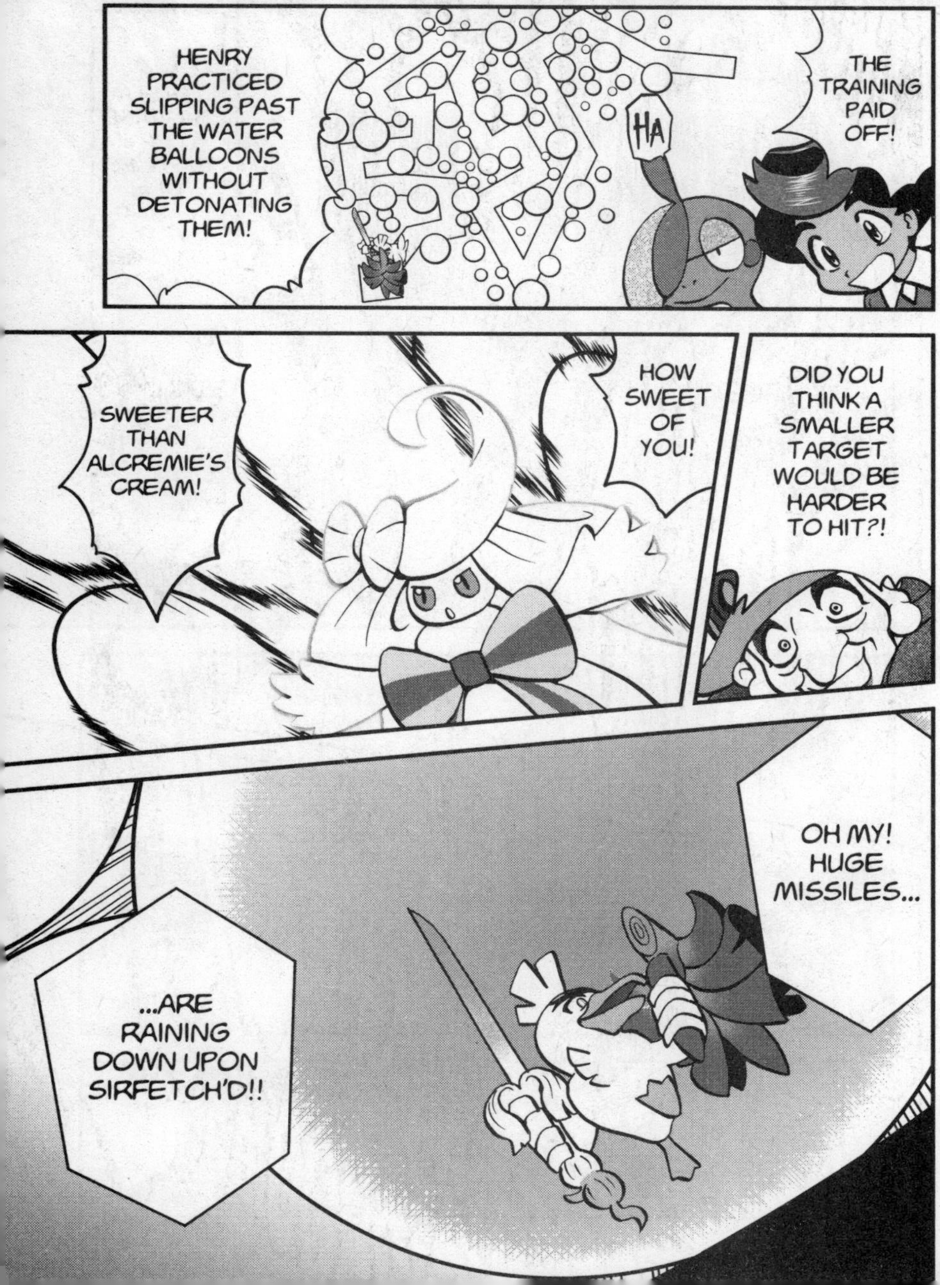
THE TRAINING PAID OFF!
HA
HENRY PRACTICED SLIPPING PAST THE WATER BALLOONS WITHOUT DETONATING THEM!
DID YOU THINK A SMALLER TARGET WOULD BE HARDER TO HIT?!
HOW SWEET OF YOU!
SWEETER THAN ALCREMIE'S CREAM!
OH MY! HUGE MISSILES...
...ARE RAINING DOWN UPON SIRFETCH'D!!

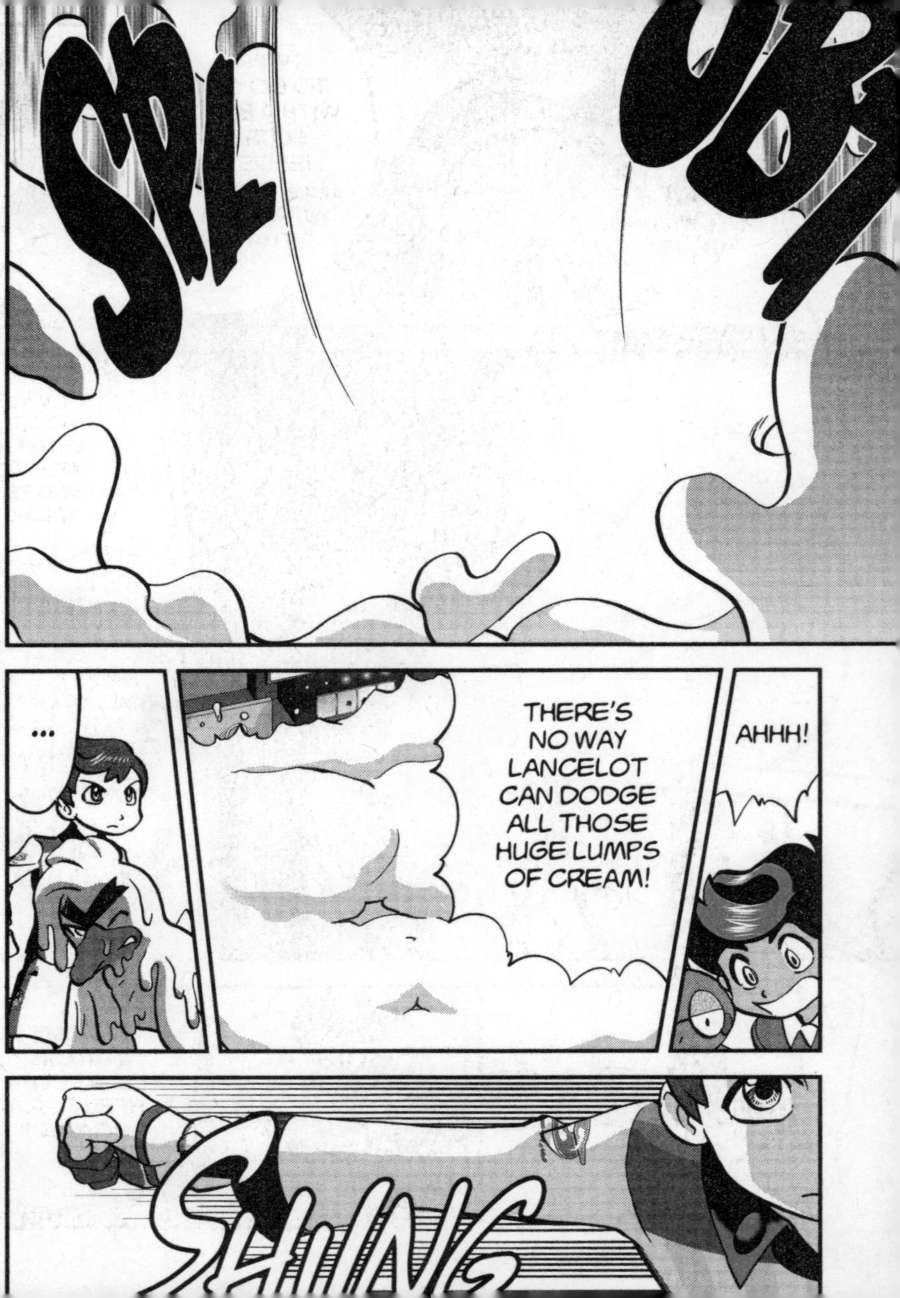
SPL
AHHH!
THERE'S NO WAY LANCELOT CAN DODGE ALL THOSE HUGE LUMPS OF CREAM!
...
SHING

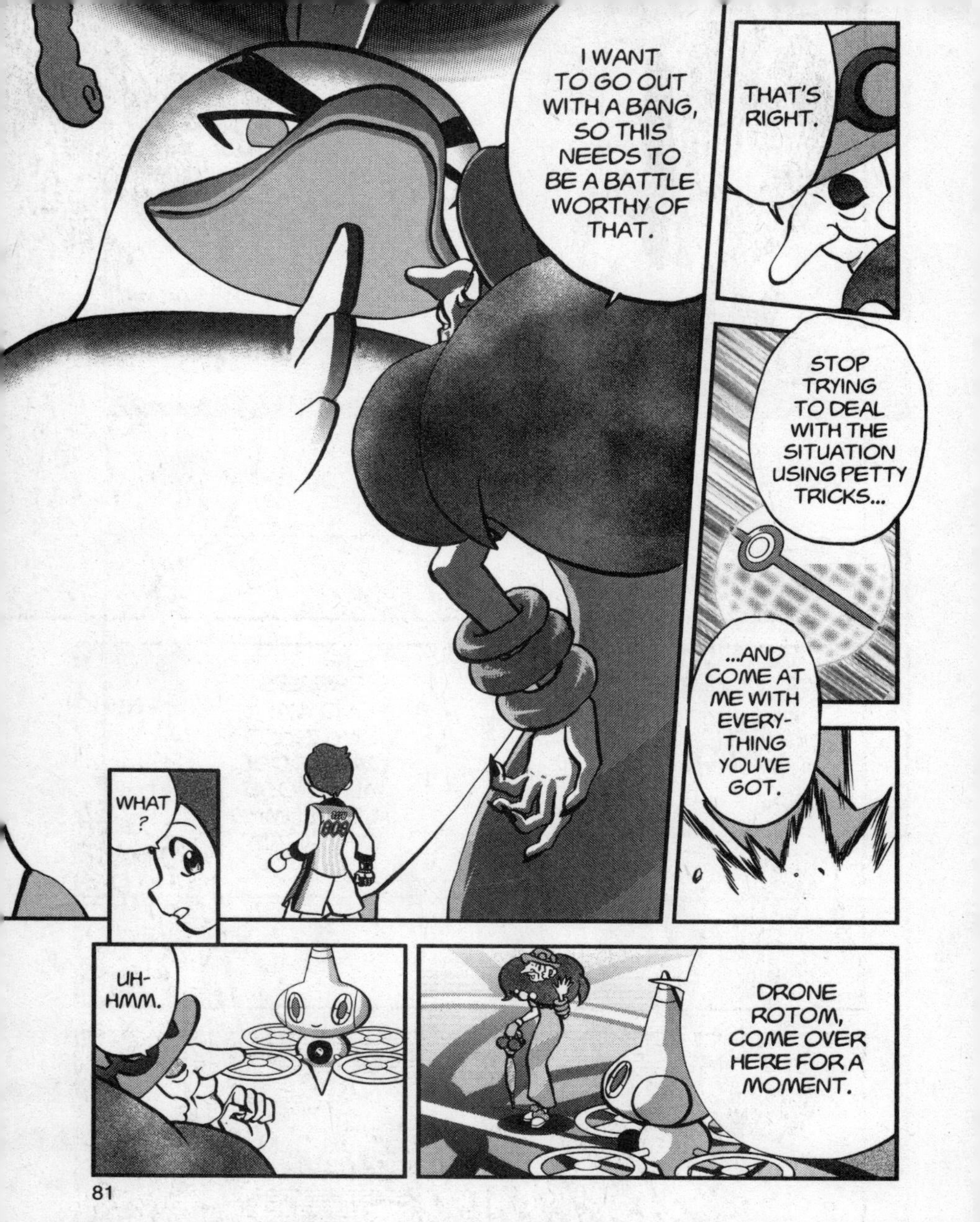

THAT'S RIGHT.
STOP TRYING TO DEAL WITH THE SITUATION USING PETTY TRICKS...
...AND COME AT ME WITH EVERY-THING YOU'VE GOT.
I WANT TO GO OUT WITH A BANG, SO THIS NEEDS TO BE A BATTLE WORTHY OF THAT.
WHAT?
DRONE ROTOM, COME OVER HERE FOR A MOMENT.
UH-HMM.

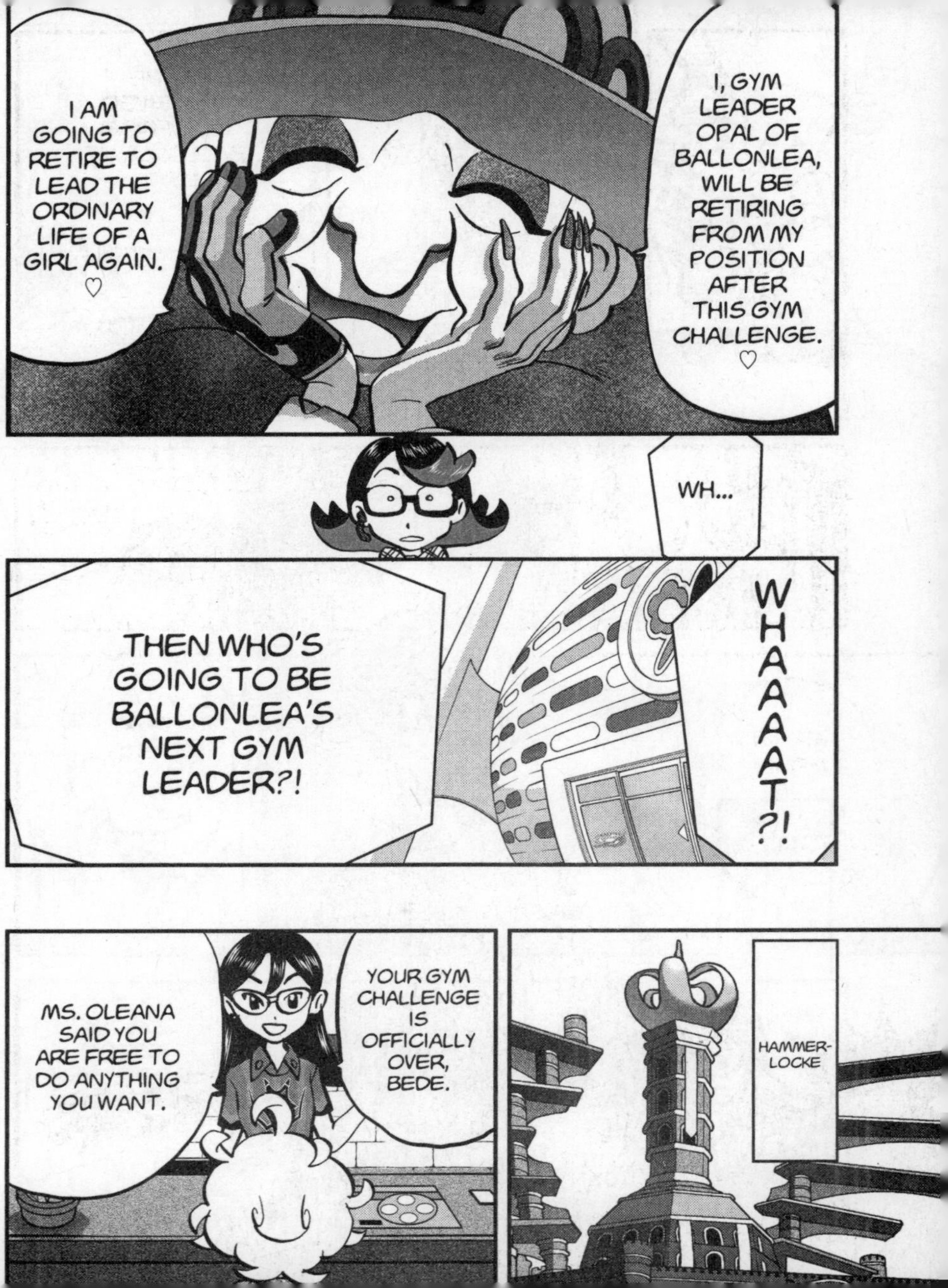
I, GYM LEADER OPAL OF BALLONLEA, WILL BE RETIRING FROM MY POSITION AFTER THIS GYM CHALLENGE. ♡
I AM GOING TO RETIRE TO LEAD THE ORDINARY LIFE OF A GIRL AGAIN. ♡
WH...
WHAAAAAT?!
THEN WHO'S GOING TO BE BALLONLEA'S NEXT GYM LEADER?!
HAMMER-LOCKE
YOUR GYM CHALLENGE IS OFFICIALLY OVER, BEDE.
MS. OLEANA SAID YOU ARE FREE TO DO ANYTHING YOU WANT.

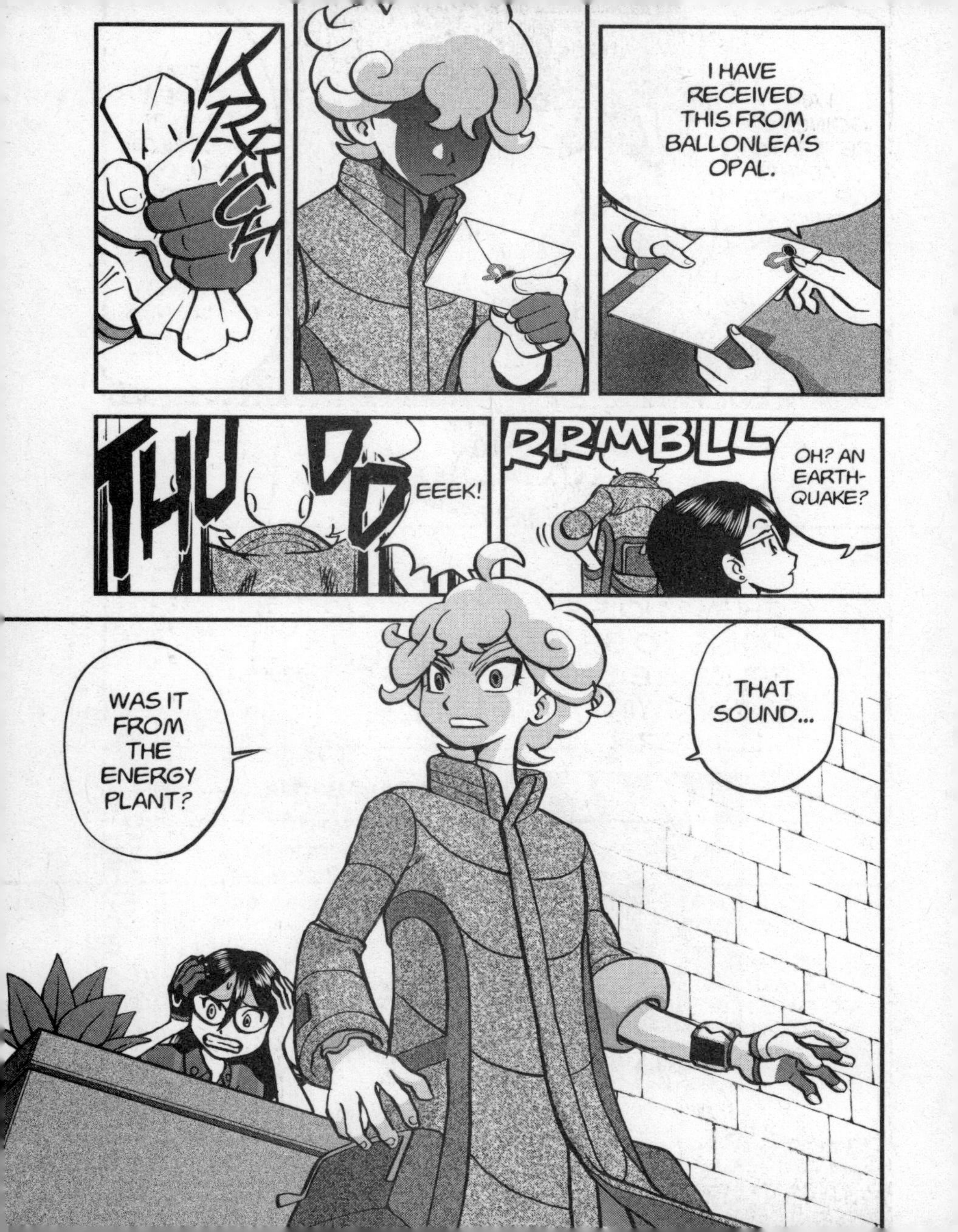
I HAVE RECEIVED THIS FROM BALLONLEA'S OPAL.
OH? AN EARTH-QUAKE?
RRMBLL
THUD
EEEK!
THAT SOUND...
WAS IT FROM THE ENERGY PLANT?

THE SECRETS OF DYNAMAX, PART 13

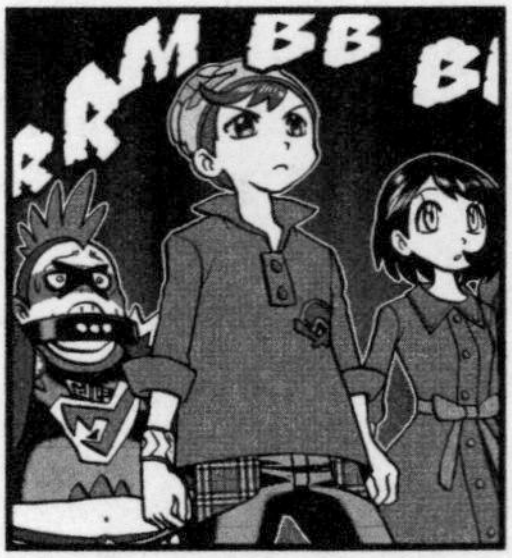
RRM BB

▲ **Up to four Trainers can participate. It's best to team up and cooperate!**

Max Raid Battle

A battle in which several Trainers face a Dynamaxed Pokémon inside a Pokémon Den.

Hidenori Kusaka is the writer for *Pokémon Adventures*. Running continuously for over 20 years, *Pokémon Adventures* is the only manga series to completely cover all the *Pokémon* games and has become one of the most popular series of all time. In addition to writing manga, he also edits children's books and plans mixed-media projects for Shogakukan's children's magazines. He uses the Pokémon Electrode as his author portrait.

Satoshi Yamamoto is the artist for *Pokémon Adventures*, which he began working on in 2001, starting with volume 10. Yamamoto launched his manga career in 1993 with the horror-action title *Kimen Senshi*, which ran in Shogakukan's *Weekly Shonen Sunday* magazine, followed by the series *Kaze no Denshosha*. Yamamoto's favorite manga creators/artists include FUJIKO F FUJIO (*Doraemon*), Yukinobu Hoshino (*2001 Nights*), and Katsuhiro Otomo (*Akira*). He loves films, monsters, detective novels, and punk rock music. He uses the Pokémon Swalot as his artist portrait.

Pokémon: Sword & Shield
Volume 5
VIZ Media Edition

Story by HIDENORI KUSAKA
Art by SATOSHI YAMAMOTO

©2022 Pokémon.
©1995–2021 Nintendo / Creatures Inc. / GAME FREAK inc.
TM, ®, and character names are trademarks of Nintendo.
POCKET MONSTERS SPECIAL SWORD SHIELD Vol. 3
by Hidenori KUSAKA, Satoshi YAMAMOTO
© 2020 Hidenori KUSAKA, Satoshi YAMAMOTO
All rights reserved.
Original Japanese edition published by SHOGAKUKAN.
English translation rights in the United States of America, Canada, the United Kingdom,
Ireland, Australia and New Zealand arranged with SHOGAKUKAN.

Original Cover Design—Hiroyuki KAWASOME (grafio)

Translation—Tetsuichiro Miyaki
English Adaptation—Molly Tanzer
Touch-Up & Lettering—Annaliese "Ace" Christman
Design—Alice Lewis
Editor—Joel Enos

The stories, characters, and incidents mentioned
in this publication are entirely fictional.

Printed in the U.S.A.

Published by VIZ Media, LLC
P.O. Box 77010
San Francisco, CA 94107

10 9 8 7 6 5 4 3 2 1
First printing, December 2022

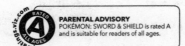

PARENTAL ADVISORY
POKÉMON: SWORD & SHIELD is rated A
and is suitable for readers of all ages.

viz.com

Coming Next Volume

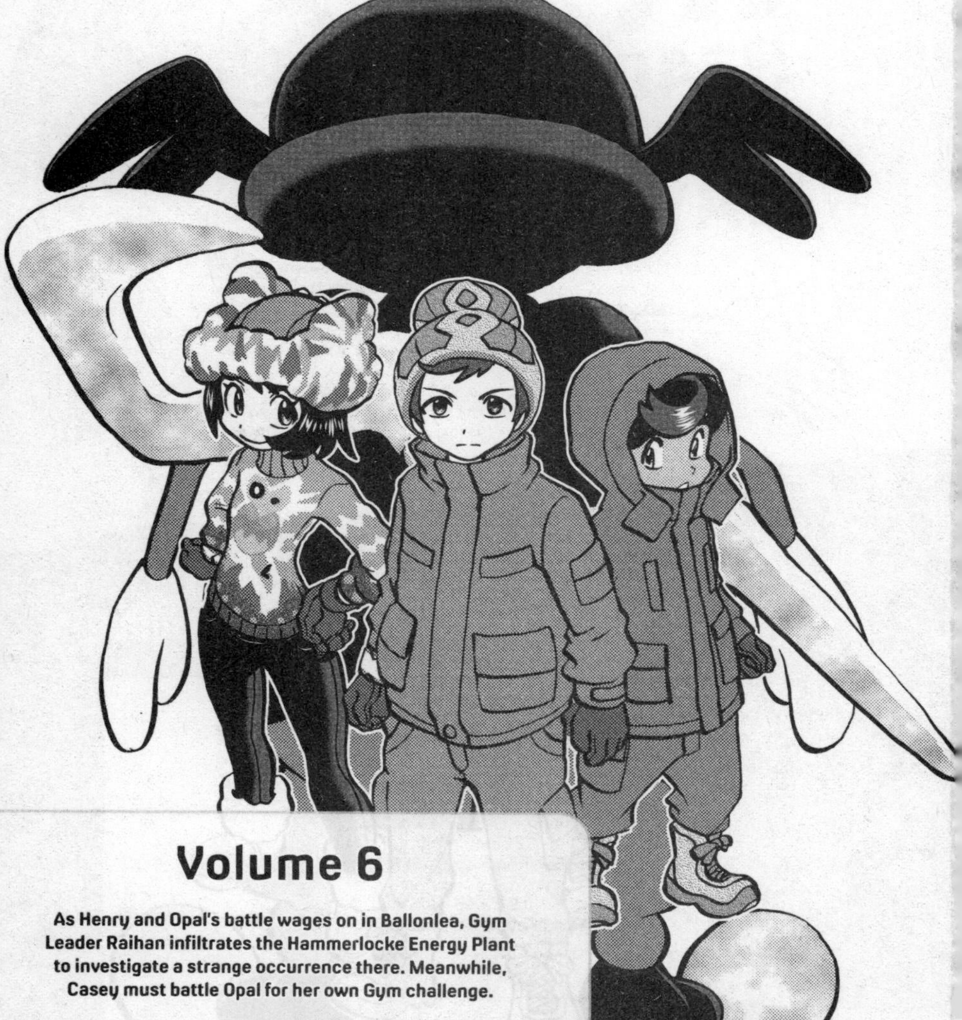

Volume 6

As Henry and Opal's battle wages on in Ballonlea, Gym Leader Raihan infiltrates the Hammerlocke Energy Plant to investigate a strange occurrence there. Meanwhile, Casey must battle Opal for her own Gym challenge.

Is there really a Dynamaxed Pokémon in the Route 9 Tunnel?!

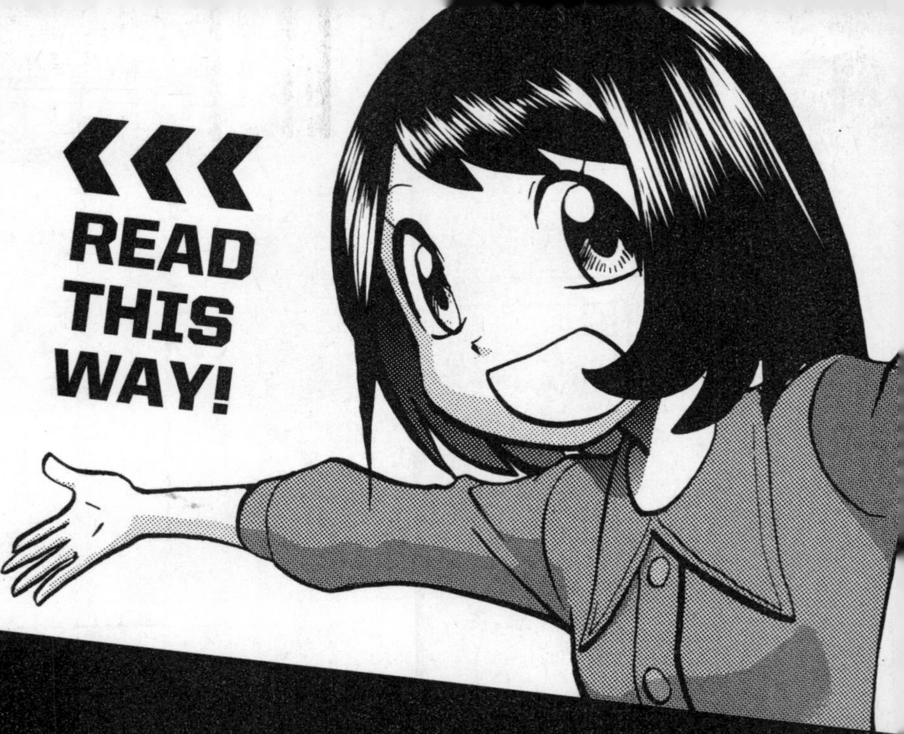

READ THIS WAY!

THIS IS THE END OF THIS GRAPHIC NOVEL!

To properly enjoy this VIZ Media graphic novel, please turn it around and begin reading from right to left.

This book has been printed in the original Japanese format in order to preserve the orientation of the original artwork. Have fun with it!

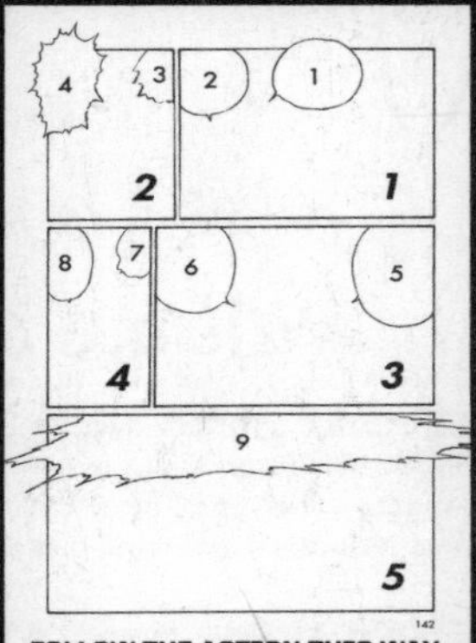

1
2
3
4
1
2
5
6
7
8
3
4
9
5
142

FOLLOW THE ACTION THIS WAY.